RITA HERRON

HAVE GOWN,
NEED GROOM

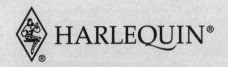

HARLEQUIN®

TORONTO • NEW YORK • LONDON
AMSTERDAM • PARIS • SYDNEY • HAMBURG
STOCKHOLM • ATHENS • TOKYO • MILAN • MADRID
PRAGUE • WARSAW • BUDAPEST • AUCKLAND

Recycling programs
for this product may
not exist in your area.

ISBN-13: 978-0-373-36258-5

HAVE GOWN, NEED GROOM

Copyright © 2001 by Rita B. Herron

www.eHarlequin.com

Printed in U.S.A.

RITA HERRON

Award-winning author Rita Herron wrote her first book when she was twelve, but didn't think real people grew up to be writers. Now she writes so she doesn't have to get a *real* job. A former kindergarten teacher and workshop leader, she traded her storytelling to kids for romance, and now she writes romantic comedies and romantic suspense. She lives in Georgia with her own romance hero and three kids. She loves to hear from readers, so please visit her Web site at www.ritaherron.com.

To all the sisters and mamas and grandmamas
who hold families together through their
family traditions. And especially to my own mom,
who spent numerous hours sewing handmade quilts
for each of her grandchildren. You gave them something
to treasure forever—your love in the shape of a blanket
to wrap around them and remind them of family.

Chapter One

"Okay, who ordered the male stripper?" Hannah Hartwell glared at her two younger sisters, Mimi and Alison, as the six-foot hunk Zorro ripped off his cape and flung it toward the leather side chair. Instead of meeting its mark, the black scrap of fabric snagged the bouquet of condom balloons dangling from the ceiling of her apartment and waved at her like a bat's wings. The surprise bachelorette party had definitely been a…surprise.

The music accompanying Zorro's striptease grew louder and the roomful of females cheered. Hannah groaned. Enthralled in the show, her sisters ignored her question. Either that or they didn't want to 'fess up.

Mimi tucked a wad of dollar bills into the waistband of Zorro's black tights while gyrating her hips to the beat of the Spanish guitar. Hannah squeezed her eyes shut. If her fiancé, Seth Broadhurst, found out about this evening, he would be mortified. A calm, practical psychiatrist, he avoided attention and wasn't a jokester like some of the other doctors at the hospital where they both worked. And she desperately wanted to maintain her hard-earned reputation with the ER staff.

Exhaustion pulled at her. She had to get some sleep. Her wedding was only a few hours away, her future teetering on the brink, just like Zorro's underwear dangling from the edge of her light fixture. Hannah waved her hands and lowered the volume of the music to a soft hum. "This was great, girls. I appreciate all the gifts, but the party's over."

A few moans accompanied her statement, but her friends conceded, offered congratulations on her upcoming nuptials, then hugged her goodnight.

Mimi sighed dramatically as the guests left. "Geez, sis, I wish you'd loosen up. Can't you go with the flow just once in your life?"

Maybe I could if you'd act responsibly just once in your life. "I can go with the flow," Hannah protested.

Mimi merely laughed, making Hannah feel incredibly boring, while her youngest sister, Alison, escorted the stripper to the door. When Alison returned, she sank onto the sofa beside Hannah.

Mimi's shark's-tooth earrings clinked as she gyrated her hips to the music again. "Wow, he had the biggest—"

"Mimi!" Hannah covered her ears with her hands, cutting off her sister before she could launch into a graphic description. So, the man *had* great muscles and sexy pecs and the biggest—

"Eyes. I was going to say the biggest bluest eyes, but he *was* well—"

"—proportioned," Alison interjected.

"—endowed," Mimi finished with a mischievous laugh.

Hannah leapt from the champagne-sticky sofa, gathering up the empty wine and champagne bottles. Punch cups, wineglasses and leftover hors d'oeuvres covered her clawfoot table, scraps of wrapping paper littered her

Queen Anne chair and cake crumbs clung to the plush velvet of her Victorian sofa.

"You can't tell me you *didn't* enjoy the guy's moves, Hannah?" A note of pure horror darkened Mimi's husky voice as she poured herself more champagne.

"He was pretty buff." Alison's cheeks flushed to a rosy glow, but her gleaming brown eyes reflected the devil brewing in her thoughts. "Getting married doesn't mean you're dead. Lighten up." Alison snatched the stripper's thong from the chandelier. "Want to keep this as a memento of your last night as a free woman?"

"You could handcuff Seth to the bed on your honeymoon," Mimi suggested wickedly as she played with the present she'd given her sister.

"You're both hopeless." Hannah pointed a manicured nail as she spoke. "You will drool after anything in pants, Mimi. And you, Alison Hartwell, are still in college. You're way too young to be thinking such naughty thoughts."

Mimi shook her long auburn hair free from its jade clasp, running her fingers through the unruly mass of curls. "Are you worried boring old Seth won't be able to get you excited like that guy did tonight?"

"You know sex is a very important part of marriage," Alison added.

"And if Seth isn't satisfying you—"

"I never said Seth didn't satisfy me!" Hannah howled, wondering if she should admit to her sexless life with her fiancé.

No, her relationship with Seth was perfect. She did not want excitement.

Before she could elaborate, the doorbell rang. "Please, pleeease don't let that be Seth." Hannah yanked the condom balloons from the ceiling then struggled to put them in the closet. "Hurry, help me hide all this stuff!"

Alison slid the handcuffs under the sofa cushion while Mimi sauntered to the door and opened it. A tired-looking trucker dressed in grubby coveralls towered over Mimi's petite five-two. His name tag read Mountain Trucking. Hannah sighed in relief.

"I have a special delivery here from Rose Hartwell," he said in a mountain drawl. "Would have been here sooner, but my truck broke down."

An almost reverent silence descended upon the room, obliterating the party atmosphere. At seventy, Grandmother Rose was the matriarch of the Hartwell clan. For years after the girls' mother had deserted them, Grammy had jumped in to help fill the parental shoes. The girls loved her dearly.

"One of you Miss Hartwell?" The trucker's gaze landed on the remainder of the decadent cake shaped like a man's body part, and his gray eyebrows shot upward.

"Yes." Hannah and her sisters nodded in unison. Alison signed the delivery slip, stepping aside as the man pushed a big box inside. He left with a chuckle.

"I bet it's the hope chest Mom told me about," Mimi said. "The grandmother of the Hartwell family traditionally passes on a hope chest to each of her granddaughters before she marries."

Hannah bristled at the reminder of their mother. She'd finally broken down and invited her mom to the wedding, hoping for a reconciliation, but she had declined, only cementing the wall between them with another foot of concrete—and the realization that her mother hadn't wanted her. Forcing herself to forget the familiar hurt, she studied the package. Her grandmother tended to be eccentric. What would she have put in the chest? Nothing alive, she hoped...

"Hurry, open it," Alison said.

Hannah took a deep breath and tore the wrapping, then opened the box, gasping in delight. A beautiful gold embossed chest sat inside. "It's exquisite."

"The chests are supposed to be replicas of the one our great-great-great grandmother brought over from England," Mimi explained.

Hannah ran her finger along the ornate decorative carving. "This chest will look perfect at the foot of my bed."

"I can't wait to see what Grammy enclosed," Alison shrieked.

Her hands trembling with excitement, Hannah slowly opened the chest and lifted a sheet of pale yellow stationery.

My dearest, loving, Hannah,

You are a very special granddaughter because you were the first miracle in the Hartwell family. You represented love and hope.

But you are the one who remembers the problems; the one old enough to realize that when your mother walked away she wasn't coming back. And with your own little heart bleeding, you were the one to square your shoulders, console your heartbroken father and nurture your little sisters. And you never complained. You showed us strength when we thought we had none left.

You are studious and smart, dependable and responsible, but cautious to a fault. Don't forget how to dream, my dear Hannah. Learn to take chances, laugh and have fun. I wish for you happiness, true love and a man who will give you all the joy a partner can.

Love you always,
Grammy Rose

P.S. Inside you should find something old, something new, something borrowed, something blue.

Hannah wiped tears from her cheeks as she laid the letter aside and gently lifted a porcelain bride doll from the chest. Something new—a new doll for her collection.

Memories of her ninth birthday surfaced, bombarding her with emotions. She'd collected dolls as a child and had received a beautiful storybook Sleeping Beauty for her birthday. But the celebration had been ruined when her mother decided she couldn't hack married life any more. All of Hannah's silly childhood dreams had disintegrated when her mother had left, closing the door behind her. Hannah had packed away all her dolls and hadn't touched them since; didn't her grandmother remember?

Swallowing back the painful emotions, she searched the hope chest, surprised when her fingers brushed something hard. A plain brown rock, slightly jagged in shape, was wrapped in the hem of the doll's lacy dress. It toppled into her hands, along with a note. "'Don't let the man you marry weigh you down,'" she read aloud. "Why on earth would Grammy write something like that to me?"

"Maybe she thinks Seth is too much of a drag," Mimi joked.

"Very funny. Seth is a pillar of the community. He's the most solid, stable man I know, something this family needs more of." Hannah unwrapped the tissue paper covering her next surprise. "Oh, my goodness, it's Grammy's bridal gown. It's beautiful."

"Something borrowed," Mimi murmured as they all admired the lacy dress.

Tiny pearls formed a border along the edge, the lace billowing out in sheer white folds. The neckline curved and slipped off the shoulders for a dramatic effect. Hannah pictured her grandmother wearing the gown at her own wedding, and a warm feeling washed over her. "This is so sweet, but didn't Grammy realize I already have a wedding dress?"

Mimi laughed. "Grammy must be getting senile."

"What should I do?" Hannah asked. "Seth helped pick out my dress."

"Wear it and save this one for your own daughter some day."

Hannah nodded and removed a pale blue garter from the chest. The girls laughed as she slipped the lacy garment over her thigh.

"Now, something old," Mimi said. Hannah's breath caught at the last item—a velvet ring box. She and her sisters exchanged animated smiles.

"I wonder if it's *the* ring," Mimi said.

"What ring?" Alison asked.

"The ring Grammy told us about when we were little," Hannah explained. "An antique pearl ring with tiny gold leaves on each side—"

"There's a legend that accompanies the ring," Mimi cut in. "The legend says that if a woman wears this pearl ring to bed the night before her wedding, she'll dream about the man she's meant to marry."

Hannah slowly opened the box, and all three of them gushed, "It *is* Grammy's pearl. Oh, my gosh, the ring is lovelier than I remembered." She traced a finger over the delicate setting, half afraid to slip the heirloom on her finger. "You guys don't believe any of those silly superstitions, do you?"

"No, but Grammy Rose does," Mimi said. "She said she wore the ring and dreamt of Gramps the night before their wedding."

Alison's eyes sparkled with excitement. "Are you going to wear the ring to bed, Hannah?"

Hannah studied the antique gold band, the tiny diamond chips set inside the rich gold leaves, the perfect pearl. "I don't know. All that legend stuff is kind of spooky."

"Don't be silly, I think it's romantic," Alison said.

"Since Seth didn't even give you an engagement ring, you can wear this one instead," Mimi said.

"I didn't want an engagement ring," Hannah clarified. "We both decided to be practical and opted for simple gold wedding bands."

"Well, when I get engaged, I want a ring," Mimi said. "A big gorgeous diamond."

"Go on, Hannah, try on the pearl, let's see how it looks on your finger," Alison said.

Hannah hesitated. "Let me get ready for bed first." Exhausted, she stood and gathered her things. "You guys can clean up, the bride-to-be needs her beauty rest."

Her grandmother's gown swished as she draped it over her arm and carried the satin-lined hope chest to her bedroom. Tomorrow her entire life would change. She'd marry Seth and have the safe, secure life she'd always wanted. She'd become a Broadhurst, a member of one of the most prominent families around, finally free of the crazy Hartwell image.

Their father, Wiley, owned a chain of used-car lots

across the country and was famous for his wacky commercials. As a child, Hannah had loved the kooky ads, but when she grew older, her dad's flamboyant tastes had brought ridicule. His embarrassing advertisements had been one reason her mother had left him.

Hannah gently spread the bridal gown over the chaise in the corner of her room, placed the bride doll on top of the chest, then placed the velvet ring box on the mahogany nightstand beside her bed. Memories of her grandmother's eccentric but lovable ways filled her thoughts as she brushed her teeth and prepared for bed. Seconds later, she donned a nightgown, then slipped back to the bedroom. Pausing to admire the pearl ring, she silently laughed at the idea of the silly legend. Should she wear the ring to bed and see if the legend came true?

Nah, the legend was just an old wives' tale.

She turned off the lamp and crawled into bed then closed her eyes. But sleep eluded her and worry set in. What if she didn't make a good wife? What if she was more like her mother than she'd thought? What if she'd made a mistake in choosing her mate or had trouble committing, like her mother?

She flipped on the light and glanced at the ring. She didn't believe superstition. But moonlight streamed through her window illuminating the perfect creamy pearl, the tiny diamonds glittering like teardrops in the centers of the leaves. Oh, what the heck.

She stared at her bare left hand, the ringless finger. Maybe she would let the pearl serve as her engagement ring. What could it hurt? Smiling to herself, she lifted the ring and slipped it on her left hand, then crawled under the covers, and pulled them to her chin. Forget the superstitious family legend. Tonight she'd sleep like the dead.

Either that, or, if the legend came true, she'd dream about her future husband. Maybe they'd even be dreams of the hot honeymoon night to come. She closed her eyes—yep, she could already see Seth Broadhurst's face in her mind.

His smoky gaze and the hunger in his solemn, brooding look was almost painful in its intensity. He swept her back with his hands, not bothering to disguise the tormented longing in the almost animal-like sound that erupted from deep in his throat. Hannah whimpered and leaned into him, unable to suppress the erotic tremors his heated touch drew from her tender skin.

He was her destiny. The man she would marry, the man to whom she would give her heart, body and soul for eternity.

Long, tanned fingers tormented her as he gently glided his fingers along her cheekbone, traced the curve of her chin. He kissed her tenderly, almost reverently, his lips a loving reminder of the words they'd shared only hours earlier when they'd spoken their vows. With a sigh of contentment, he pulled her into his embrace, murmuring heartfelt words of love and need that would forever be imprinted in her brain. Hannah curled into his warmth and strength, savoring the way he clung to her as he carried her over the threshold to their home.

Moonlight danced through the lacy curtains creating a halo around his magnificent form, shimmering streaks of gold through his thick dark hair, highlighting cheekbones etched in granite, a smile that barely made it to his lips, the strong jaw that remained clenched as he fought for control. Her gaze played over his broad shoulders, down his washboard stomach, then he turned to undress and she noticed a small crescent-shaped quarter-moon birthmark on his hip.

Moments later, they consummated their marriage with a passion unlike anything she'd ever imagined. He emanated strength, power; a man who would protect her and take care of her. And when she stared into his handsome, rugged face, she knew that after their honeymoon night together, they would forever be bound as one.

Hannah awoke with a start, streaked with sweat and tremors of unsated desire that shook her to the core. The sheets lay tangled around her aching limbs, the pearl ring glistening in the moonlight, the pillow beside her empty. A frustrated sigh tore from her lips as she realized she was alone, that the passionate union had been a dream.

She touched the unbroken circle of the ring's band, the silly legend echoing through her mind. *If you sleep wearing the ring the night before your wedding, you'll dream about your future husband.*

She dropped her face into her hands and groaned, a ball of confusion knotting her stomach. What was she going to do? She had dreamt all right—only Seth, her fiancé, had *not* been the man in her dreams.

Chapter Two

"I can't marry Seth today." Hannah inhaled a deep breath, but the waistline of her wedding gown was so tight it was cutting off the oxygen to her brain. Why else would she be dizzy?

Because she was having a severe case of cold feet minutes before her wedding.

Making matters worse, her father had pulled another one of his stunts—newspaper reporters and a TV crew had joined the guests to film every second of her ceremony. She *had* to go through with the wedding. Piano music wafted through the church signifying the seating of the guests.

"Of course you're marrying Seth." Mimi gestured toward her pale-green bridesmaid's dress. "I'm not wearing this hideous chiffon thing for nothing. It makes me look twenty pounds heavier than I already am!"

"You're not fat and you know it." Alison rolled her dark brown eyes heavenward. "You have a beautiful hourglass figure most women would die for."

"Yeah, you're busty," Hannah added, glancing down in despair at her own rather puny chest. Even with her new bra, she barely had cleavage. "I'm just not sure about me and Seth," Hannah confided in a low voice.

"What if he's the wrong man for me? Grammy Rose met Seth last Christmas, what if she *knew* when she sent me that ring?"

"That's crazy," Mimi said.

"You know Seth is the right man for you. In here." Alison curled her hand into a fist and pressed it over her heart.

Trouble was, she didn't know. Hannah had long since forgotten childish dreams of love and romance. Her marriage to Seth was based on friendship, a mutual, almost business-like agreement they'd decided on months ago, thinking their professional relationship made them a suitable match.

Hannah gulped. Her brain whispered she'd be a fool not to marry Seth, he'd give her the stable, secure life she'd always dreamed of. But her body screamed for more: the heat, the raw hungry looks, the frantic, urgent coming together—the dark, virile man in her dreams. And her heart confused her even more, whispering that the man in her dreams was her soulmate. Foolish nonsense. She and Seth were soulmates, weren't they?

She rubbed her temple where a headache had started pulsing. They were definitely…friends. And they'd almost made love a couple of times, but she'd backed away, claiming she wanted to wait until they were married. What if the real reason she'd held back was because there'd been no spark, no sizzle? What kind of marriage would they have together without passion? Without true love.

"Last night I dreamed I was making love to a stranger," Hannah admitted in a strangled voice. "Why would I dream about another man when I'm marrying Seth?"

Mimi threw her hands in the air dramatically as she

spun around to face Hannah. "Because Seth isn't the kind of man who conjures up erotic fantasies."

Alison narrowed her eyes at Mimi in a warning, then laid a comforting hand on Hannah's shoulder. "Hannah, everyone has crazy dreams. They don't always have to mean something."

"Do you think I'm making a mistake?" Hannah asked.

"I think *anyone* getting married is a mistake," Mimi replied dryly.

"Just because Mimi is anti-marriage doesn't mean you can't be happily wed," Alison said softly. She handed Hannah her bridal bouquet, a huge assortment of white lilies with rose-colored satin ribbons streaming from the center. Hannah sniffed at the arrangement, the fragrance so sweet it made her eyes water.

"But what about the dream and the legend of the ring?" Hannah's chest tightened. "I was supposed to dream about the man I was going to marry."

"Maybe it was your way of having one last fling before you're tied down to Mr. Boring," Mimi offered with a devilish smile

Alison sent Mimi another warning glare and straightened the lace on Hannah's neckline. "Silly folktale."

Still unconvinced, Hannah remembered the dream kiss and knew in her heart she couldn't hurt Seth by marrying him if she really didn't love him. Her mother's parting words rose to haunt her. *I only married you, Wiley, because I was pregnant. A real marriage needs more…*

Her parents had married because of her. Hannah definitely wasn't pregnant, but had she agreed to marry Seth for the wrong reasons? For security, not real love. "Go tell Seth to come here."

"But it's bad luck for him to see you before the ceremony," Alison argued.

"I don't care. I have to talk to him."

Mimi nodded and rushed out while Alison fanned Hannah's face to calm her. Seconds later, Seth bobbed his sandy-blond head in, his expression perplexed.

His face fairly faded in front of her eyes, the shapely square jaw and chiseled face of the man from her dreams invading his space like a surreal sci-fi movie— *Invasion of the Body Snatchers.*

Like a flash of heat lightning, the vision disappeared and Hannah gaped at Seth, wondering why he fell vaguely short of her erotic fantasy. A woman's toes should curl and her blood should boil when the man of her dreams kissed her, right? A woman should burn at a man's touch. Maybe that passion was what her mother had been missing with her dad. She couldn't marry Seth and repeat her mother's mistake. She had to know now.

"What is it, Hannah? Did you forget something?" Seth asked.

Hannah framed Seth's face with her hands and kissed him fervently on the mouth. Her toes would curl, her blood would sizzle, the passion would come, the hunger would surge. Magic would happen just like she'd dreamed when she was a little girl.

She kissed him harder.

Burn, baby, burn.

But her toes didn't curl. Didn't even twitch.

Her blood didn't boil. Didn't even bubble.

Darn.

At best, she was lukewarm.

The startled gasp that erupted from Seth's throat when she finally ended the kiss didn't sound like hunger or passion or even surprise. And her bright-red lip-prints streaked his mouth.

"I—I have to know something, Seth," she whispered, near panic. "Do you have a birthmark on your b-behind?"

Seth stumbled backwards, his eyes dilating. "What?"

"A little quarter-moon?" She pointed to his left hip. "Up here, on your left cheek?"

Seth's Adam's apple bobbed up and down, steam practically oozing from his ears. "No. What's come over you, Hannah? You're acting odd."

An overwhelming sense of panic hit her. "Seth, tell me why you want to marry me."

His eyebrows narrowed. "What?"

"Please, just tell me. Why do you want to marry me?"

He ran a hand through his hair, spiking the ends. "We talked about this before. We make a good match, Hannah. We work well together. Have the same goals. We're both doctors."

"What about passion?" Hannah asked, desperate for something to cling to.

His face flushed. "I…I thought we decided sex could wait. That passion wasn't really important."

No, but love was.

"Seth, do you love me?"

He chewed the inside of his cheek. "I…I care about you…"

"But you don't really love me," Hannah finished for him.

"We'll have a good life, Hannah. We work well together, we're compatible—"

"I'm sorry, Seth." Tenderly, she laid her palm on

his cheek. "Maybe we were wrong. Maybe passion is important."

He shook his head. "Can't we discuss this later? The guests are here, the preacher. We have cake, we have a schedule...."

Typical, all business, no emotional response.

The vision of the other man appeared again, briefly but intensely, and she blinked Seth back into focus, a sickening knot balling in her stomach. Yes, Seth was the wrong man for her— No toe-curling or blood-boiling kisses. What if she married him, had children, then discovered they'd made a mistake? She never wanted to put a child through a divorce—not after the pain she'd experienced. And if she didn't love Seth passionately, it wouldn't be fair for her to marry him. He deserved better.

"I'm sorry, but I can't marry you, Seth. You're a wonderful guy, but you deserve a woman who loves you with all her heart and soul. And I deserve a man who feels the same way. I..."

Hannah spotted her sisters hovering at the door. "I'll go tell Dad," Alison whispered.

"I'll tell my parents," Seth said tightly.

Hannah reached for Seth's hand. "No, I'll do it."

Raising her head up high, she snatched the tail of her dress and marched to the church entryway. Cameras, guests, her father, Seth's parents—all stared back at her. The organist's eyebrows shot up as if to signal it was time for the wedding march. A reporter started running toward her, his camera angled to catch her face. On his heels, a half a dozen others seem to come out of the woodwork, camera lights flashing.

Hannah panicked and blurted out the announcement, "I'm sorry, everyone. We've called off the wedding."

A gasp rumbled through the room, Wiley shot forward, Mrs. Broadhurst jumped up and shrieked, and Hannah swung around and stumbled toward the back door, searching for an escape. Alison and Mimi stood at the side door, waving her forward. She darted past Seth, who scowled at her, and jogged outside, scanning the parking lot for her car before remembering she'd left it at her house. Mimi had driven her over. The honeymoon getaway car, a white Cadillac convertible complete with clanking cans and streamers, winked at her in the sunlight. Hannah darted toward it.

The last thought she had before she climbed inside the plush white interior was that later that night she would see herself on TV. Everyone had black sheep in their family, but the Hartwells had a whole flock of weirdos grazing the southeast. Uncle Elroy had served a stint in prison, Aunt Betty-Jo was a kleptomaniac, cousin Wally claimed he'd been an ostrich in a former life…the list went on and on. She'd spent her adult life trying to overcome her infamous family image.

But now her worst nightmare had come true—Hannah Hartwell, respected doctor and hater of public scenes, had just become another Hartwell spectacle.

DETECTIVE JAKE TIPPINS was having a terrible, no-good, very rotten day. As paramedics lowered his gurney from the ambulance to the ground outside Sugar Hill General, a camera flashed and he ducked his head. Damn. He couldn't even hide his humiliation. He'd been shot in the butt, the EMTs had shredded the seat of his jeans, exposing his backside for the whole world to see, and now the media had jumped on the bandwagon, wanting the story. Thank God the hospital banned the vultures from entering the ER. They might blow his cover at Wiley's.

He scrubbed a fist over his stubbled jaw, then dropped his forehead on the gurney as the EMTs quickly pushed him through the doors and wheeled him toward one of the exam rooms. Pain shot from his hip down his leg like a razor blade. Still, he reached behind him to try to cover his wound with his hand. A man had a right to a little privacy, didn't he?

"BP high. One-fifty over ninety. Respiration twelve and even. Pulse eighty-eight and steady," the EMT called.

The nurse pulled the sheet down around his knees and lifted the bandage. A gust of cold air hit his backside. "Still bleeding."

He gritted his teeth as she applied more pressure to his wound, then tried to cover himself again. To think that the day had started out so simple. Most of the employees at Wiley Hartwell's used-car lot had taken off early to attend the wedding of Wiley's oldest daughter, Hannah. Wiley lived and breathed for his kids. He had boasted nonstop about his daughters ever since Jake had come to work for him, so Jake felt as if he knew them. But he didn't get that whole hoopla about family stuff himself; he'd grown up being shuffled from one place to another, without a mother or father to speak of, and he was used to being alone. Weddings to him signified the death of a man's bachelorhood, his whole identity. No wonder the groom partied the night before and wore black to the ceremony.

To avoid the uncomfortable formality, he'd volunteered to man the car lot during the wedding, hoping to take advantage of the opportunity and sneak into Wiley's office. But after Wiley'd left, some punk kid had tried to steal a sports car right off the lot, and when Jake had tried to apprehend him, the black-leathered twerp had shot him. The reporters had dogged him from the site of the shooting at breakneck speed, calling him a hero.

A heavy-set nurse began to fire insurance questions at Jake, taking his medical history. A second nurse checked the bandage, tsking under her breath. "I need to get you another IV, sir." He nodded as she left the room, then lifted his weary head and glanced through the glass-topped doorway on the opposite side of the room. He could swear he saw a beautiful blonde streak right past the window then dart into the room across from him—wearing a full-length wedding gown. She looked like an angel. Or maybe a princess.

Nah. No princesses or fairy tales in the real world. He closed his eyes, giving in to the fatigue. He must be seeing things.

Hell, he might even be delirious.

HANNAH BREATHED a sigh of relief to find the locker room empty. She quickly shed her wedding dress and crammed it into her locker. It actually felt good to pull on fresh scrubs and her lab jacket. That gown had felt like a straitjacket.

She grimaced. Her wedding gown shouldn't have felt confining; it should have felt magical. She fought the tears, but they trickled down her face anyway. What in the world was wrong with her? She wasn't the emotional type. She hadn't cried since she was nine, not since that awful birthday when her mother had left.

Maybe she'd suffered some sort of breakdown, a post-traumatic reaction to her parents' divorce. Maybe she needed therapy. First she'd deserted Seth. And now she'd shown up at work where she would have to explain why she wasn't at her wedding marrying him. Why the heck had she come to the hospital?

Because it seemed like the safest place, she acknowledged silently as she searched for a tissue. Her family would be calling or dropping by her house to check on her, and Seth might show up demanding to talk. She wasn't ready to deal with any of them.

Besides, she *had* heard the news of a car crash on the radio while she'd been driving around in circles trying to decide what to do. There'd been a shooting mentioned, also, although she'd only caught the tail end of that story. The hospital probably needed her. Work was the one place she'd be able to forget about her messed-up personal life and feel responsible again.

She leaned against the locker, trying to collect herself as the shock of her own actions settled in. She hoped her sisters would have explained to their father....

Finally gaining control of her emotions, Hannah inched open the door and winced at two reporters still hovering in the hallway like starved lions sniffing out their prey, ready to pounce for the kill. She hadn't expected them to follow her to the hospital. Sometimes she hated living in a small town—the reporters would have a heyday with the story, the traditional wedding gone awry, prominent doctor jilted at the altar. She pictured the headlines and groaned—Wacky Wiley's Wacky Wedding.

She loved her father, but he was a sucker for publicity. Unlike her, he thrived on attention and had probably already twisted the entire fiasco into a scheme to sell more cars. Poor Seth. Guilt dug into her conscience like a razor-sharp scalpel. She would never forgive herself for hurting him. He must absolutely hate her.

And his mother would probably sue her if the story appeared on the society page, tainting their blue-blood family name. As for her family, she'd simply fallen into footsteps already molded by other Hartwells. Twenty years of trying to overcome her roots down the drain because of a thirty-second decision.

She closed her eyes and allowed the regret to flow, along with the heartache she assumed would follow from losing Seth. Even if she changed her mind and crawled back on her hands and knees groveling, his family would probably never forgive her. Oddly, heartache for Seth never came—only sadness for embarrassing him. And the ball of fear that had lived within her since she was a little girl swelled inside her again. She'd inherited her mother's blond hair and fair skin. Maybe she was like her mother in other ways, too.

Disgusted with herself, she sniffled and dried her cheeks with the hem of her jacket, reasoning the only way to avoid the press was to throw herself into work. She peeked through the door again, grateful the reporters had disappeared.

A surgical scrub hat pulled over her hair for disguise, she fielded her way to the nurses' station. Tiffany, the big lovable nurse who ran the floor, paused near the curtained partitions and sent her a gap-toothed smile.

"What are you doing here, Dr. Hartwell? I thought you were getting married today."

"I canceled the wedding," she said, striving for a confident voice.

Tiffany's chubby face reddened in surprise.

"You mean you're not marrying Dr. Broadhurst?" Susie, one of the physicians' assistants, hesitated over a tray of medicine. "But he came by this morning on the way to the church."

"I know," Hannah said. "It didn't work out." She shrugged and hurried over to Tiffany, unable to think of an explanation that sounded rational. "I heard about the car crash and thought you might need some help. How many victims?"

"Six." Tiffany narrowed her eyes. "But if you're upset, you don't have to stay, we'll manage. We've already marked you off the calendar for the next week."

"I'm fine." Hannah shifted uncomfortably. "I'd really like to work."

Tiffany nodded, tactfully choosing not to press the issue. "All right. Doctors Bentley and Douglas are with the car victims."

Hannah tried to steady her voice. "What else do we have?"

"A gunshot wound in three. Man was shot in the posterior. I paged Dr. Hunter but he's in surgery with a ruptured spleen."

"Oh, yes, I heard about the shooting on the radio, too." Hannah reached for his chart. "What are his vitals?"

"Blood pressure's a little high. EMTs applied a pressure bandage, started a drip. His name's Jake Tippins." Tiffany quickly recited his other vital signs. "I suppose you're aware the shooting occurred at your daddy's car lot."

Hannah's gaze swung up in shock. "No…what happened?"

"Someone tried to steal a car. Our patient caught him." Tiffany gestured toward the outside waiting area, wiping a pudgy hand across her forehead. "The reporters are calling him a hero. I had to chase 'em away from the ER."

Hannah silently groaned, felling empathy for the

man. The six o'clock news tonight would be full of Hartwell happenings. "Has his family been notified?"

"Man claims he has no family. Didn't want us to call anyone."

Once again sympathy for the man filled her. "Okay. I'll take care of him."

Tiffany nodded, checking the other charts. "I'll assist you in a minute."

Hannah headed to the exam room, then slipped inside. The man lay face down, his head propped on his left hand, his breathing steady as if he'd fallen asleep. Or maybe he was unconscious. She scanned his chart and noted that his vitals were still stable. He'd lost some blood, so he'd probably given in to fatigue. She studied his back, her gaze traveling the length of his long body to where his toes hung off the end of the gurney. He was one of the biggest men she'd ever seen. Thick black hair covered his head, and his wide shoulders and firm, muscular arms attested to the fact the man worked out. Probably lifted weights, or maybe he was a body builder…when he wasn't selling used cars.

He'd been wearing jeans, but the seat had been cut away. A sheet lay draped across the lower part of his body, and his hand clutched it over his buttocks. She fought a chuckle. Even in sleep, the man still clung to his dignity.

She inched the sheet down and her gaze slid lower to assess his wound. He roused slightly. "Sir, I'm Dr. Hartwell. I'm going to examine you now."

He mumbled something incoherent, still half asleep. Even so, his fingers momentarily tightened around the sheet. "Relax, Mr. Tippins, I'm not going to hurt you." She slowly pried his fingers from the material. The paper-thin elastic gloves popped against her wrists as she prepared to do a preliminary exam. Striving to be gentle, she pushed his denim shirt out of the way, removed the pressure bandage then dampened a cotton swab with antiseptic.

He moaned and stirred, his hand swinging around to cover his wound once more. She shook her head as they played tug-of-war with the sheet.

"Mr. Tippins, just lie still please. I have to examine you."

His head bobbed up and down in concession, but the way his shoulders straightened signaled he'd braced himself for more pain. And his hand tightened around the covers jerking it over his backside again. This was getting ridiculous.

"Uh, Mr. Tippins, I can't help you if I don't examine the injury."

He made a noncommittal noise which sounded faintly like a swear word, then slowly released the back of the sheet and buried his head in his arm. Hannah almost laughed, but caught herself. Poor man, if he was shy, she certainly wouldn't make things worse by making some silly comment about the location of his injury.

She pressed the area around the bullet wound to measure how deeply it was embedded, putting pressure at different points. The bleeding had stopped, the skin yellow...

"Ow." He flinched.

"Sorry, Mr. Tippins. I'm almost finished."

His head bobbed again, and she patted the area with the cotton swab, wiping away the dried blood.

"Great place to get shot, wasn't it?" His voice rumbled thick and low, almost gravelly. "I feel like Forrest Gump."

"I can't think of a good place to get shot," Hannah said dryly, a smile twitching at her mouth.

"Think I'll make it?"

He was joking, a good sign. "You'll be fine." She tossed the cotton swab into the trash.

"You're going to have to put me under the knife, aren't you?"

Hannah sighed. Men could be such babies. Even the big muscular ones. "If you're asking if the bullet will have to be removed surgically, then yes. It's embedded a good four to five inches."

"Will you do the surgery?"

"Yes. If they're short in surgery I'll probably assist. We're a small town facility here." Hannah heard his sigh and her defenses rose. "Do you have a problem with female doctors, Mr. Tippins?"

"No," he muttered. "Not as long as they know what they're doing."

She stiffened. Was he insinuating she didn't? "I can assure you I'm well trained. I completed a surgical rotation last month before I joined the ER. I'll be gentle, too, I promise."

"Oh, your hands are great, Doc, it's not that."

Hannah shook her head, exasperated, finally deciding the pain must be affecting his brain. "Then what is it, sir?"

He exhaled, his body rumbling with his breath. "I just don't like hospitals, that's all."

"Not very many people do," she said sympathetically. She spotted an unusual-looking bruise and leaned closer to examine it. "Hmm."

"I hate it when doctors go 'hmm.'"

Hannah chuckled. "Sorry. It's nothing really. I noticed a small dark spot. Thought it have been an exit wound but it's not.''

''Probably a bruise, I went down pretty hard on a tire iron when that creep shot me.''

She peered closer, contemplating thanking him for what he'd done for her father, but suddenly realized the bruise was a small birthmark. A crescent-shaped, quarter-moon birthmark. Right on the arch of his hip.

Her chest tightened—she'd seen that birthmark before. ''It can't be,'' she whispered.

His head snapped up. ''What's wrong, Doc?''

She hadn't realized she'd spoken out loud.

He angled his head slightly to look into her eyes and for the first time, Hannah saw his face. ''It can't be what?''

His dark gaze locked with hers, the pupils of his eyes slightly dilated, the unmistakable cleft in his chin hauntingly familiar. Hannah staggered backward, a bolt of heat engulfing her as if an inferno had burst into flames at her feet. She recognized this man. She knew him…*intimately.* He was the tall, dark handsome man from her erotic dreams.

His heavy-lidded, dark-brown eyes paraded over her, a sliver of need sizzling in the luminous depths. The room began to spin crazily, and the day's events crashed to a sudden mortifying halt.

Jake Tippins moaned, and she quickly glanced back down to see if he was okay, but the room rocked sideways. Hannah clutched the bedrail to steady herself, but her legs faded into numbness and the spots that danced before her eyes emerged into one big black hole. She'd never fainted in her life, but she recognized the symptoms. Just before she passed out, she tried to warn her patient to roll out of the way.

Chapter Three

What the hell?

Jake gritted his jaw in pain when the dreamy looking woman suddenly staggered and reached for the gurney. He twisted sideways to catch her, but the IV limited his movement, and she collapsed beside him on the floor.

"Help! Someone help me! Nurse, hurry, the doctor passed out!"

His gaze zeroed in on her name—Dr. H. Hartwell. He'd thought that's what she'd said, but he'd been so sleepy he'd figured he'd heard wrong. Hannah Hartwell was Wiley's daughter. What was she doing in the ER? She was supposed to be at her wedding. "Someone get a doctor!" he yelled again.

Impatience flaring, he climbed awkwardly from the gurney, grappling with the IV pole as he knelt to take her pulse. Thank God she was breathing. A sprig of baby's breath protruded from her surgical cap, and her eyes looked slightly red and swollen. He pushed off the cap, revealing wispy blond hair. Yep, it was the same woman he'd seen in the wedding gown. So, he hadn't been delirious.

"Dr. Hartwell, wake up," he whispered, panic hitting him. Had Wiley heard about the shooting and ordered

Hannah from her wedding to take care of him? Was that the reason she'd been upset?

Her cheeks seemed pale, long blond eyelashes lying on her creamy skin like thin layers of cornsilk. And her slender body was way too still for comfort.

Suddenly the nurse appeared, her eyes widening in dismay. "What in the world…?"

"She passed out," Jake explained. "I've been yelling for help."

A tall, older physician with a scowl on his face stormed into the room. Jake watched helplessly as they settled Hannah Hartwell onto a gurney and wheeled her away.

"I…WHAT happened?"

"You passed out on us, Doc," Tiffany said. Hannah tried to get up, but Tiffany pressed a gentle but forceful hand on her arm. "Relax. You need to lie still and let us check your vitals again."

Hannah bit back a moan, mortified. "I'm fine, really, Tiff. I just need something to eat." *And to figure out what's happening to me today.*

The chief of staff frowned. "Dr. Hartwell, I don't understand what you're doing here, or why you dragged all these reporters along—"

"I'm sorry, I didn't mean for them to follow me," Hannah said weakly.

Dr. Porter pursed his thin lips. "Need I remind you this is a hospital? We're here to treat patients, not flaunt our personal escapades."

Hannah opened her mouth to respond, but he silenced her with a lethal look. "We can't allow anything, especially our personal lives, to affect our work here or to jeopardize the safety and health of our patients. Is that understood, Dr. Hartwell?''

The seriousness of his words brought a wave of shame to her. ''Yes, perfectly,'' Hannah whispered.

''Then I suggest you go home until you've had time to recover, and let this…this circus you've created die down.''

Hannah nodded, biting her lip as her superior turned and strode from the room. Tiffany patted her arm sympathetically. ''We'll get you something to eat, Doc. You're not going anywhere until I know you're okay.''

Hannah's heart squeezed at Tiffany's unusual show of concern. She'd witnessed the woman mothering some of the young nurses but had never been on the receiving end of such treatment. Hannah had always been the caretaker. She didn't like this vulnerable feeling. ''I'm fine, really, Tiffany. I need to see about that patient.'' Worry assaulted her. ''Please tell me I didn't pass out on top of him.''

Tiffany laughed. ''No, on the floor.''

''Thank God.''

''But Mr. Tippins climbed down and took your pulse while he yelled for help.''

''Great, the patient doctoring the doctor.'' Hannah put her hand across her forehead. ''I hope he didn't injure himself further.''

''Mr. Tippins looked like a pretty tough man to me. I think he'll be all right.'' Tiffany checked her watch. ''Dr. Hunter should be removing the bullet just about now.''

Hannah accepted the juice Tiffany offered, deciding she'd rest for a few minutes, but only until Jake Tippins made it to recovery. Then she'd visit the man, apologize and beg his forgiveness. And she'd find out if she'd been hallucinating when she'd examined him. He simply couldn't have a birthmark like the man in her dreams.

Because bizarre things like this didn't happen to her.

Mimi, maybe.

But not stable, secure, hardworking, levelheaded, mature Hannah.

"WELL, that just about covers it." Hannah avoided Jake's hard gaze as she instructed him on activities to avoid during recovery. "Do you understand, Mr. Tippins?"

"Yeah," he said, his voice slightly slurred from the medication.

Tension knotted Hannah's shoulders. "On behalf of my father, I want to thank you for catching that thief. And I want to apologize for fainting on you."

"It was no big deal." Still lying on his stomach, he propped his face on his hand and looked up at her, a goofy grin on his face as if he sensed her awkwardness. Either that or the pain medication had affected his brain.

The chief of staff's warning rang in her ears. "Well, I truly am sorry."

"No problem, Doc."

But she did have problems. Somehow she had to forget that she'd seen this man's naked backside in her dreams. And that the very reason she'd canceled her wedding and jilted her fiancé at the altar was because of the erotic dream she'd had about *him*.

Back to business. She had to salvage her reputation. She might have lost Seth and the Broadhurst name, but she couldn't lose her job. And if she didn't start acting more professionally, she probably would do just that. "How are you feeling now, Mr. Tippins?"

"Just peachy," he said in a deep drawl. "How about you?"

Hannah tucked a strand of hair behind her ear, her fingers trembling. "I'm fine." *Just coming down with a case of the Hartwell crazies.*

"Your color's looking better."

Hannah averted her eyes, lifting the bandage slightly to check his incision. "Are you in pain?"

"I was earlier, but you distracted me."

Hannah resisted the urge to pinch him and wipe that cocky grin off his face. "That wasn't my intention, I can assure you. It's been a hectic day, and I hadn't eaten anything. I'll definitely be more careful from now on and watch my blood-sugar level."

He rolled his shoulders in a slight shrug. "Ahh gee, and here I thought I was special."

The man was incorrigible.

Ignoring him, she said, "Get some rest tonight. We should be able to release you tomorrow."

He must have been exhausted because he simply nodded and smiled tightly. His only sign of pain—the muscles in his cheeks clenched when she retaped the bandage.

Hannah swallowed, stunned by the sudden hot sensations weaving through her. Maybe her hormones were out of whack. Coupled with nerves, an imbalance could cause hot flashes. She should check her estrogen levels, although she was way too young for—

"Doc?"

She signed off on his chart. "Get some rest now, Mr. Tippins. I need to check my other patients."

"Aren't you supposed to be on your honeymoon?"

Hannah paused, absentmindedly tapping the chart

with her pen. "How did you know I was getting married?"

"Wiley let everyone at the dealership off early to attend your wedding. That's the reason I was working by myself."

Right, he worked for her father; how could she forget? Maybe if there'd been someone else working with him he wouldn't have been shot.

Something else for her to feel guilty about.

His fingers brushed over her knuckles. "Did I say something to upset you?"

Hannah pulled her hand away, her eyes glued to his long tanned fingers. "I…er, I didn't get married today."

His dark eyebrows lifted slightly over high cheekbones. "I could have sworn I saw you in a wedding dress. Must have been hallucinating from the pain."

"No, I was wearing one when I arrived," Hannah admitted, figuring he'd hear the news from the car-lot grapevine. "I called off the wedding."

A streak of surprise lit his sleepy, bedroom eyes. "That's too bad."

She arched a brow at him. He didn't sound as if he thought it was bad at all. And he was a stranger; she didn't owe him an explanation.

"I'm sure my dad will come by to thank you for your heroics," she said, reverting back to their earlier conversation.

A brooding expression tightened the lines at the corner of his mouth. She'd run out on a good, stable man because she'd dreamt of this stranger?

Forget hormone pills. She should call the men in the little white coats to come and haul her away. Maybe she needed to see a psychiatrist. Except Seth was the best psychiatrist in town and she had a feeling he wouldn't be sympathetic.

She suddenly felt dizzy again.

"Tell your dad he doesn't need to come by," Jake mumbled in a low voice.

"What?"

"I'm no hero, Dr. Hartwell. Catching that guy was a freak thing."

Hannah frowned, confused by the intensity of his words. She needed to get away from this man, and fast. Something deep and troubled lurked in the depths of his eyes. Something dangerous and dark that called out to her.

Something that scared the life out of her.

"I need to see those other patients now." Without waiting for a reply, she backed toward the door, fighting the urge to touch the man's broad shoulders and remind him he was a hero. But the memory of the erotic dream floated around her, the warmth in her belly sending a sliver of uneasiness up her spine. She must have seen Jake before, probably at her father's dealership. Subconsciously she'd found him physically attractive and conjured him in her dream. Simple.

End of story.

The dream wouldn't come true. Even though the man was sexy as homemade sin, she'd never ever in a cajillion years become involved with a used-car salesman. Especially one who worked for her lovable but notoriously outlandish father.

JAKE GROANED, his brain foggy from the sedatives the nurses had administered, his thoughts registering the fact that Hannah Hartwell had canceled her wedding. There had to be a story there; one Wiley would probably embellish when he dropped by to visit. Had the woman's poor fiancé cheated on her or done something equally heinous to make her dump him? If so, Wiley would be ticked.

Like a vision, she glided out the door. Her lithe figure disappeared just as a plan formulated in his mind. Wiley had boasted about Hannah's intelligence, and Joey DeLito, Wiley's top salesman, commented that she'd helped him with his books a few times. Perhaps she knew something about her father's business that could aid his investigation. He'd been searching for a way to embed himself in the Hartwell family. Her sister Mimi was dating Joey, so he couldn't move in on her. And her youngest sister was too young for him. But Hannah wasn't married now or engaged; he'd use Hannah to find out more about Wiley.

Exhausted, he closed his eyes, deciding his plan to see her had nothing to do with the fact that lying face-down with a bullet hole in his backside and an IV in his arm he was rock-hard from wanting the woman.

No, it had everything to do with his job. And he'd do anything he could, use *anyone* he had to, to solve the case and get out of this little sleepy backwards town. He had to get transferred back to the city where he belonged. Where he could get lost in the endless crowds. Where he could simply exist as a number. Where he could live in peace and die the same way, without having to explain himself to anyone. He was a loner. And he always would be.

Hell, he'd learned the hard way about untrustworthy females. And obviously Hannah Hartwell fitted that description well—she'd just jilted her fiancé at the altar. He'd rather take another bullet than get personally involved with a woman like her.

Chapter Four

She must be losing her mind.

It was the only plausible reason for her to have such intense feelings about a silly dream—and such a strong attraction toward a strange man who differed so drastically from the men she normally dated.

Hannah Hartwell had always been predictable and cautious and rational—she never did anything erratic or spontaneous or...or *emotional*.

Until that dream.

She'd let that silly legend destroy her sensibleness and dictate her choice in marriage. Which meant she either needed to see a shrink or to find out if some cursed psychic power she didn't know existed ran in her family.

The answer lay with Grammy Rose.

Hannah's fingers trembled as she punched in her grandmother's phone number. Please let her be there, she prayed, her stomach lurching when the phone rang at least a half-dozen times.

Finally, on the seventh ring, her grandmother answered. ''Hello.''

''Grammy?''

''I said hello. Speak up now, my left ear's full of

dust. Herman Whitewall's been plowing up my garden and I can't see three feet in front of me or hear my own self think.''

Hannah laughed. Her grandmother must be getting senile. Herman Whitewall had passed away three years ago. ''Grammy, it's me, Hannah.''

''Oh, hello, dear. How was the wedding? I wanted to be there so badly but the doctor made me stay in bed with that cold, 'fraid I'd get pneumonia. I told him nothing could get this old lady down.''

''I didn't exactly get married, Grams.''

''Really?'' Her grandmother's tone held a hint of amusement, but not surprise.

''No. I...I called off the wedding at the last minute.''

''Decided Simon didn't light your torch, huh?''

Hannah smiled. ''No. And his name is Seth, Grammy.''

''Seth, smeth. I didn't think that man was right for you.''

''You didn't?'' Hannah's fingers tightened around the phone. ''Why not?''

Her grandmother made a chortling sound. ''Woman ought to light up when the man she's going to marry walks in the room, and frankly, honey, you didn't. But don't worry, you'll make a beautiful bride some day. When the right man comes along, of course.''

Hannah twisted the phone cord in her fingers. ''Grammy, I appreciate the hope chest you sent me and all the nice things. Your gown was beautiful, but I have to know—are you psychic?''

''Heavens, no.'' Her grandmother chuckled. ''I wish I was. I'd win the lottery and buy myself a fancy cane and some new teeth.''

Hannah smiled, mentally adding the cane to her

Christmas list. She took a deep breath, and her gaze automatically landed on the pearl ring. "If you aren't psychic then, I need to ask you about the ring—"

"What did you want to know, dear?"

"Did you wear the ring and dream about Grandpa the night before your wedding?"

Grammy Rose's soft laughter echoed over the line. "Lordy, did I? Honey, it was X-rated. I woke up in such a sweat I had to go out and buy new bloomers."

Heat climbed Hannah's neck. Her father had definitely inherited his outrageousness from Gram—maybe senility and eccentricity ran in the same gene pool. "Really?"

"It's the truth or my name ain't Rose Hartwell." Her grandmother paused, lowering her voice as if inviting Hannah to share her confidence. "Did you dream about somebody, Hannah?"

Hannah's throat clogged. "Uh...yes."

"The man in your dream wasn't Seth, right?"

"How did you know?"

"Destiny."

Destiny? "I don't think so. He's totally wrong for me."

A shriek of laughter burst through the phone. "Heavens, honey, you can't fight it. Now tell me about this man. How did you two meet?"

Hannah relayed the episode at the hospital, describing Jake's injury and her fainting spell. Her grandmother listened, occasionally mumbling, "Mmm-hmm."

"Actually I think I must have seen him at the car lot before, but we weren't introduced. His face must have gotten stuck in my mind and he suddenly appeared in my dream."

"Love at first sight."

"No," Hannah said emphatically. "*If* I saw him, I barely even noticed him."

"When do I get to meet your new young man?" Grammy asked as if she hadn't heard Hannah's protests.

Hannah rolled her eyes at her grandmother's enthusiastic tone. "He's not my new young man. He's a used-car salesman who works for Dad. And he's all wrong for me." But Grammy Rose continued to ask her questions, and Hannah continued to deny her attraction to Jake. A half hour later, Grammy Rose hung up, sounding as smug and satisfied as if she'd just played matchmaker. Hannah stared at the ring, more confused than ever. She must be losing her mind—her grandmother's exuberance had almost swayed her into believing the legend might be true.

Ridiculous.

She tugged off the ring and laid it on the table, the diamonds glittering beneath the light. Silly folktales didn't come true. And she wouldn't allow it to affect her rational judgment any more than it already had.

She should wear the ring, she thought, with a twinge of nerves gnawing at her. She'd never been a defiant person, but she'd defy the legend.

Determination filling her, she picked up the ring and slid it back on her left hand. There. The room didn't spin, dishes didn't start flying off the shelves, no genies suddenly appeared from any bottles.

Feeling relieved, she decided she must be having some kind of temporary meltdown. She'd heard residents, especially ER physicians, suffered from stress. The doorbell rang, and Hannah jumped, confirming her diagnosis.

Mimi rushed in. "Dad's on his way. I just thought I'd warn you."

Hannah gripped the door. "Thanks. Was he upset?"

"Not upset, really. Just worried about you, sis. Are you okay?"

"Yes, I think so." Hannah's mind reeled with all the miscellaneous wedding details she'd left for her father to straighten out. How could she have been so irresponsible? Not that she thought she'd made the wrong decision in calling off her wedding, but why couldn't she have seen the truth sooner? "What…what did Dad do about all the food, the cake…"

"You know Dad," Mimi said with a light laugh. "He invited all the guests to have refreshments anyway."

"Oh, God. What did Seth's parents do?"

"They left in a huff," Mimi said. "Dad said he planned to take the rest of the cake and punch to the car dealership for a commercial, then serve it to his customers. The reporters loved the idea. Josephine— that lady from the *Gazette*—promised she'd stop by and grab some pictures."

Hannah laughed in spite of her misery. "Leave it to Dad to find an advertising venue for wedding cake."

"I suggested he freeze some of the leftovers for Thanksgiving."

"You're kidding?"

"It would save us some cooking," Mimi said, her tone serious.

"I'd rather have one of your specialty desserts from the coffee shop, Mimi. I don't think I want reminders of today's events on Thanksgiving. Hey, did you take Alison back to school?"

"I just got back. She—"

The doorbell rang and Hannah tensed. "That's probably Dad."

"Good luck, Hannah." Mimi paused. "And, sis?"

"Yeah?"

"For what it's worth, I think you did the right thing today. You and Seth…well, he seems like a nice guy, but you two just didn't seem suited."

Hannah brushed a tear from her cheek, thanked her sister, then followed her to the door. She honestly thought she'd done the right thing, too. For both her and Seth.

So why did her spontaneity and newfound freedom suddenly scare the bejeebies out of her? And why had her grandmother sounded so confident, as if the legend was bound to come true?

JAKE CLUTCHED the covers in his fist as he awakened, the sharp sting of his nightmares still fresh on his mind. The drugs maybe?

No. Not this time.

Darkness draped the hospital room in a cloak of loneliness.

He fought off the familiar anger, focusing on the present. Why had the dreams returned from his childhood to haunt him now? Because he was alone?

Hell, he'd always been alone. He *liked* being alone.

Jake Tippins was a die-hard cop who didn't need anyone. He'd been on his own since he'd turned fourteen and his father had stalked off in a drunken fit and never returned. Oh, his mother hadn't been too devastated. She'd been a beautiful blond temptress who hadn't gotten her kicks from raising a kid. And she didn't like to be alone.

Ever.

She'd entertained one man after another until Jake had grown sick of being invisible and abandoned and had found his own way—into a life of crime. Stealing cars.

How ironic—now he was a cop assigned to uncover a major car-theft ring, probably based at Wiley Hartwell's used-car lot. And Wiley's daughter, the woman he'd decided to use to speed up his investigation, was a beautiful blond princess.

No, not a princess. A beautiful blond temptress. Hell, the woman was sexy enough to make him want to strip off his clothes, with or without a medical exam.

She'd jilted one man today—would she move on to another target tomorrow? The answer had better be yes or his plan would fail.

Jake grimaced as he recalled Wiley's earlier visit. His boss had stopped by to thank him for being a hero, but Jake had pretended to fall asleep while the man expounded on his heroics. He didn't want thanks for doing his job, especially when he lied to the man repeatedly. Not only lied, but investigated him.

Sometimes undercover work sucked.

He rolled to his side, groaning, half in pain, half in frustration as he remembered the gentle way Wiley's daughter had tended to his wounds, the sweet honeyed scent of her shampoo, those pale gold eyelashes fluttering like a curtain over her remarkable blue eyes. For the first time in his life, he felt a nudge of something like hope stir to life.

If everything Wiley Hartwell said about his daughter proved true, her sprint from the altar today had been out of character. He half hoped the good doctor would prove the rest of his theory wrong too, about her and her father. But he knew she helped her father with his books sometimes, giving her the perfect opportunity to manipulate the numbers. And her sister Mimi was so tight with Joey, she might be his accomplice.

If he discovered Wiley was running a car-theft ring, he'd have to arrest him. And if Wiley's beautiful daughter Hannah or her sister Mimi were involved...

HANNAH STIRRED sugar into her father's coffee and handed him the mug, aware he'd been watching her ever since he'd walked through the door. She only wished he'd changed from his garish gray tux. Simply looking at his pink ruffled shirt and white patent leather shoes reminded her of her earlier debacle. He'd even managed a manicure, she noted, spying a thin coat of clear polish on his blunt nails.

"Are you sure you're all right, honey?" Wiley studied her intently over the rim of his cup.

"I'm fine, Dad. So, please stop staring at me like I'm going to break apart any minute."

Wiley shoved stubby fingers through his curly brown hair, sending the unmanageable strands into disarray. His hair gel had no doubt worn off hours ago, a sign he'd repeatedly done the gesture several times today, a testament to the stress she'd inflicted on him.

Hannah sipped her own hot tea and perched on the armchair beside the fire, wondering if she should take off for a couple of weeks and let publicity die down. Only, with Wiley's latest statewide ads and her wedding disaster airing on TV, she wouldn't be able to escape the notoriety of being Wiley's daughter anywhere she went.

"I'm sorry, Dad. I didn't mean to embarrass you." Unaccustomed as she was to sharing her personal feelings with her father, she couldn't offer an explanation.

He frowned. "You want to talk about the breakup?"

She shook her head.

"Honey, I..." Her father stared into his mug as if the rich dark coffee held the answers. "I know you don't like to confide in me. I'm not sure why...."

The anguish in his voice startled her. "Dad—"

He held up his hand. "It's okay, Hannah. I'm not trying to pressure you. And you didn't embarrass me." He rubbed at his trouser leg awkwardly. "Heaven knows though, that I embarrass *you* sometimes, but I don't mean to. I love you girls. I always have."

"I know that, Dad." Tears burned Hannah's eyes. If only all the kids she'd grown up with could have seen the real man beneath her father's showy exterior, not the flamboyant TV salesman, maybe they wouldn't have teased her unmercifully. And if only she could forget the fact that his stunts *had* embarrassed her, that her mother had deserted the family because of them...

He sipped his coffee, his voice deep and husky. "Just tell me one thing—did Broadhurst hurt you?"

A smile curved Hannah's mouth. She ached to walk over and wrap her arms around her father, assure him she was okay, but for some reason, she found herself holding back, exactly as she always did when he tried to get too close. "No, Dad. I'm the one who called off the wedding."

He clenched his hand around his knee as if he wanted to reach for her but knew she wouldn't be receptive. Hannah had never been the cuddly, affectionate one— that had been Mimi. "You want to talk about it?"

Hannah sighed. "I simply realized we weren't right for each other, Dad, and I didn't want to make a mistake."

"Like I did with your mother?"

The pain-filled words hung between them, but she couldn't bring herself to voice her thoughts. "Dad—"

He gently took her hands in his and squeezed them. "I'm not trying to make things worse here. I'm behind you, no matter what you decide, honey."

Guilt suffused Hannah. She wished she knew something to say to alleviate the hurt in her father's eyes, but they had never been able to talk about her mother.

"I'm sorry I left you to handle all the details," she finally said.

Wiley shrugged. "No problem. I'm going to try to make good use of the cake," Wiley said, easing the tension his usual way, with a joke.

Hannah laughed. "I'm glad. I certainly don't want to have to eat it."

Wiley picked the newspaper off the coffee table, the small-town paper full of Hartwell happenings. News of the shooting at the car lot occupied the first page, bumping Hannah's canceled wedding and photos of her running from the church to the third.

"I heard you took care of my salesman at the hospital today," Wiley said.

Hannah's fingers tightened around her cup, the vivid images from her dream bombarding her. "Yes. Apparently he caught someone trying to steal a car."

Wiley nodded. "Yep. Tippins is a good man. A little rough with his sales technique, but he's learning."

Great. One day maybe he'd star in one of her dad's commercials.

Surely he'd be out of her dreams by then.

"I'm glad you saw him at the hospital," Wiley continued, oblivious to her turmoil. "Odd though, he didn't want any press about his heroics. Heard he even refused to give an interview for the paper."

So, maybe he didn't like a lot of attention the way her father did. That still didn't mean she and the man had anything in common.

"As a matter of fact, I wanted to talk to you about checking on him when he's released."

Hannah nearly spilled her tea in her lap. "What?"

Wiley grinned as if one of his wild brainstorms had just hit him. "Poor guy doesn't have any family. I stopped by to see him on my way over here, but he fell asleep while I was there. And I have to go out of town tomorrow. We're taping that early-bird ad for Thanksgiving in Atlanta. Maybe you could give Jake a ride home from the hospital."

Chapter Five

Jake shifted sideways in the hospital bed, unable to get comfortable. Getting shot in the butt had complicated his life in more ways than one. He might have blown his cover if his picture had appeared in the paper, and now Wiley figured he owed him. Adding insult to injury, he'd probably be sitting on one of those silly foam doughnuts for weeks.

The local sheriff, a tall man in his late fifties with a slight paunch, studied the statement he'd taken about the shooting. "Anything else you can tell me?"

"That's it. The whole thing happened in a matter of minutes." Jake glanced out the window at the countryside, frowning at the colorful array of fall leaves twirling in the wind. He'd have to take a few days off to recover, meaning he'd be staying in this little town even longer. He didn't like to stay in one place for very long, the very reason he'd opted to join the special Atlanta task force that placed undercover detectives in various hotbeds of crime. Not that sleepy little Sugar Hill, Georgia, was a hotbed of crime, but recently the suspicions about the car-theft ring revolved around the town. Stolen cars *had* definitely been moved through Wiley's lots.

"Did you question the kid?" Jake asked. "Find out what caused the punk to do something so stupid?" He considered revealing his identity to the sheriff, but decided to hold off.

Sheriff Walker shook his head in disgust. "Bunch of his buddies dared him to take the car for a joyride. Guess he freaked when you nabbed him, so he shot you."

"Stupid kid," Jake said, remembering how dumb he'd been at the same age.

"Got the gun from his dad's drawer at home." Walker made a clicking sound with his cheek. "His parents are pretty upset. They're basically good people. Maybe a little jail time will do him good."

Jake frowned. Serving time could go either way— harden the boy to crime and add another dark layer to his attitude or make him want to turn things around. Unfortunately, Jake had bigger fish to fry.

The sheriff headed to the door. "Oh, by the way, my daughter recently got her license. I think I'll stop by Wacky Wiley's. Maybe you can cut me a deal on a good used car." A chuckle reverberated from his chest. "Last year he had all his salesmen dress up like elves for the Christmas specials. Better get yourself healed so you can fit into those little green tights."

The man's booming laughter echoed off the walls as he left the room. Jake rolled his eyes, praying he'd finish his investigation before Christmas. Every job had its limits—he'd run through a jungle full of snakes, walk through fire, risk his life to keep the streets safe, but there was no way in hell he'd put on a silly elf suit.

No sooner had the sheriff left, than Jake's partner and friend, Trevor Muldoon, loped in, grinning. Although Muldoon was in his fifties, Jake admired the older man and his commitment to his job. He was also one of the few cops he'd known who'd been able to keep a family. Muldoon enjoyed dispensing advice, constantly urged Jake to search for a good woman, and bragged about the difference his marriage had made in his life. So far, Jake hadn't bought any of the malarkey. "Hey, man, how's the b—"

"Don't say it," Jake warned, knowing the older man intended to make him the butt of his jokes.

Muldoon chuckled. "The chief wanted me to find out if this shooting had anything to do with the investigation."

"I don't think so," Jake said. "The local sheriff was just here."

"Yeah, I saw him take off. I hid in the hall, didn't want anyone to see me."

Jake nodded. "Sheriff claimed the punk kid who shot me tried to steal the car on a dare. He's too amateurish to be the mastermind we're looking for. I need more time."

"We'll follow up on the kid. Chief wants you to tie this thing up before Christmas," Trevor said. "Says he'll have to pull you back in soon."

"I'll have the case solved by then," Jake said. He'd step up the investigation, use every available clue and possible resource he had.

The intercom buzzed in the hallway and a voice paged Dr. Hartwell.

Trevor frowned at the announcement. "Your doctor?"

"Yeah. You'd better get out of here, man."

"Keep me posted." Trevor slipped out the door, and Jake leaned back against the pillow. He'd been wondering where the elusive beautiful doctor had been this morning. Wiley had phoned first thing to tell him he'd enlisted Hannah to drive him home. Jake had considered telling Wiley to forget it, that he'd take a cab, but then he'd decided why not? The sooner he got to know the doc the better.

HANNAH WAS on her way to answer the page when she saw a man slip from Jake Tippin's room. Hmm, even though he didn't have family, at least he had a visitor. Not one of the salesmen from Wiley's, though. And how odd—she'd noticed the same man earlier—he'd been lurking in the hall. When the sheriff had left Jake's room, the man had slipped behind a medicine cart until the lawman had disappeared. Who was the stranger, and why wouldn't he want Sheriff Walker to see him?

The intercom announced her name again, and she shook off the uneasiness, knowing bigger problems awaited her. Having just completed an early-morning rotation in the ER, she was exhausted, but the minute she'd heard the page, adrenaline had kicked in. Adrenaline spurred by nerves. Her stomach clenched as she spotted Seth's parents enter the chief of staff's office ahead of her.

The Broadhursts were prominent retired physicians who'd donated scads of money to the hospital. They had power, influence and the backing of the board.

And they most likely hated her.

Why had she been asked to meet them in the chief's office? Had they listened to the apology she'd left on their answering machine at home and decided to confront her?

She twisted her fingers together as she stared at the closed door. They couldn't have her fired for what she'd done to their son, but they could make her life hell, could create dissension, could make her *want* to leave.

Maybe she should simply ask for a transfer. She could move to Atlanta, complete her residency at another hospital, make the situation less awkward for everyone. She'd already heard some nasty rumors floating around—she'd been having an affair, had rubbed it in Seth's face when she dumped him. In a small town like Sugar Hill where everyone knew everyone else, the gossip about her jilting Seth would linger for months.

Striving for courage, she raised her hand and knocked. Dr. Porter's curt voice invited her inside. Seconds later, she took a seat in a wing chair facing the chief of staff. Seth's parents situated themselves on the adjacent navy loveseat. To her surprise, Seth stood on the far side, leaning against the wall, looking grim.

"You're probably wondering why I asked you join us," Dr. Porter said.

"I think I have an idea," Hannah said, deciding to take a direct route. At six-three, the elderly gray-haired Dr. Porter was impressive and intimidating, not only because of his size, but because he had practiced medicine himself for years, had a reputation as a renowned surgeon, and contributed regularly to a major medical research journal. When his wife had died the year before, he'd left a prominent Boston facility to manage this small-town hospital, saying he needed less pressure.

Hannah certainly hadn't helped his situation any.

Seth's mother, an attractive brunette in her early fifties, stared blankly at her while her husband's scowl reflected his displeasure.

"I know I owe you all an apology," Hannah said, praying she sounded sincere. "I'm sorry if I embarrassed the hospital by my actions. And I'm really sorry for the way I handled things yesterday with Seth.'' She gave Seth a wary smile.

Seth nodded, his gaze oddly understanding.

Seth's mother's mouth tightened into a thin line. His father arched a bushy brow.

She directed her gaze at his parents. "I never meant to hurt Seth, I hope you two believe that. Seth is really a wonderful guy.''

"And an important part of the hospital," Dr. Porter pointed out.

"Yes," Hannah said, hearing the unspoken message, *More important than a young resident.* "He's very well respected here and I still would like to think of him as a friend. I honestly believe that I did the right thing, though, by canceling the wedding. I think one day Seth will agree.''

His arched brow said he wasn't sure, but he was contemplating what she'd said.

"You couldn't have told my son this before his wedding day?" Mrs. Broadhurst asked with disapproval.

"Or maybe like your father, you simply enjoy public displays?" Mr. Broadhurst snapped.

Hannah winced at the comment about her father, half wanting to defend him, the other half wanting to scream that she hated public displays. Surprisingly, Seth spoke, saving her from commenting.

"Mother, Dad, that's enough," Seth said. "What happened between Hannah and myself is our business. Not yours.''

Mrs. Broadhurst bristled while Mr. Broadhurst's nostrils flared.

Hannah searched for a plausible, rational approach to winning their understanding, but she couldn't think of one. She remembered the crazy dream, the legend—no, she could not tell them about the legend. They would think she'd lost her mind.

Which, of course, she was beginning to think also. Especially considering how composed and levelheaded Seth appeared in the aftermath of their canceled wedding.

Dr. Porter folded his hands on his desk and cleared his throat, cutting off her thoughts. "That brings me to the reason I asked you all to meet here. The personal lives of my staff are really of no consequence to me, Dr. Hartwell, except where their behavior affects the ethical code and the respect of other professionals. I must admit I've heard some gossip about you in the halls, and I've seen the newspaper photos."

"I'm sorry, Dr. Porter. I had no idea the reporters would mention the hospital."

"I'm concerned that this debacle might affect both your working relationships and the morale at the hospital."

Hannah chewed on her bottom lip. "I can assure you that I'll remain professional. I know I can work with Seth…" The Broadhursts shot her a stern look, "…um, with Dr. Broadhurst."

"I certainly have no problem with Dr. Hartwell," Seth said amicably.

Dr. Porter stood as if dismissing them. "Well, I, for one, thank you for your honesty, Dr. Hartwell. And I will hold you to your word. If not…"

Hannah nodded as he let the sentence trail off, wincing at his silent warning.

Seth's parents shook Dr. Porter's hand, Hannah apologized to them again, and the Broadhursts left with a brief thanks, although Hannah sensed they weren't totally satisfied. Seth's gaze caught hers, an awkwardness between them that she hated. He forced a small smile for which she would forever be grateful. Maybe they could remain friends. Maybe he would recommend a good shrink....

When the door had closed behind them, the chief of staff caught her hand. "Dr. Hartwell, you are aware how much the Broadhursts' contributions mean to this hospital?"

"Yes."

"Then I'm asking you to do everything you can to rectify your relationship with them. Do you understand?"

"Yes sir."

Hannah's stomach plummeted. She would do everything she could to smooth things over with the wealthy couple, *except* marry Seth. With a heavy heart, she slipped out the door to follow through on the promise she'd made to her father the night before.

She was going to find Jake Tippins, the man who had virtually seeped unwanted into her dreams and caused her to go crazy for a day and drive him home. And she'd have to do it without letting the man know that she'd seen him naked in her dreams. And that he was the very reason she'd called off her wedding.

JAKE RUBBED his hand over his eyes, trying to block images from his latest dream. After Trevor had left, he'd dozed off, but instead of having another nightmare about his childhood he'd had erotic dreams of sleeping with a blond vixen—Hannah Hartwell.

She'd been naked and hot and writhing beneath him.

Boy, he was in trouble.

As if temptation had his number, the good doctor

walked through the door. "Hi, Mr. Tippins, how are you feeling today?"

"Like I've been to hell and back."

Dr. Hartwell lifted a narrow blond brow. "You don't mince words, do you, Mr. Tippins?"

"No reason to," he said. "What you see is what you get." *Except for the fact that he wasn't a car salesman, he was a cop. And that he could lie at the drop of a hat.*

And he'd like to see the slender curves that lay beneath that lab coat.

Oh, hell…he wasn't handling this well at all.

"Are you ready to go home?"

"Yeah." He indicated the backless hospital gown. "Just let me grab my luggage."

A soft chuckle escaped her as she tossed a paper bag at him. "Sorry, no suitcase, but I did pick up a pair of sweats for you to wear home."

He opened the bag and peered inside at the shapeless black drawstring pants. "Thanks, Doc."

She blushed. Actually blushed. Had he ever seen a woman look so innocent and so wanton at the same time? "I didn't know your size and figured sweats would be more comfortable with the bandage."

Heat climbed his neck. "Yeah, well, this is great. Not that I haven't enjoyed giving all the nurses a thrill with this hospital gown, but I don't want to get arrested for indecent exposure."

The door opened and Wiley poked his head in the doorway. "Hey, Tippins, how're you doing?"

"Fine," Jake said.

"Can I see you a minute, Hannah?" Wiley asked.

"I thought you were out of town."

"I'm on my way, just running a little late," Wiley said.

Jake noticed Hannah's shoulders tense. She told Jake she'd be right back, then disappeared into the hallway.

Curious, Jake awkwardly climbed from the bed, dragging the gown together in the back as he hobbled over to the doorway. He peered through the door crack and saw Hannah frowning at her father. They appeared to be arguing. He tried to read their lips and thought he saw Hannah say something about the car business, that she didn't want his money. Finally Hannah slipped an envelope into her pocket with a frown. His suspicions mounted. Hannah sometimes helped Wiley with the books; was he paying her to be an accessory to a crime?

Wiley squeezed Hannah's arm and she nodded stiffly, jammed her hands in her lab-jacket pocket, then strode toward Jake's room. He scrambled back to the bed, bumped into the lunch tray and nearly broke his toe. Biting back a cry of pain, he struggled to yank on the sweatpants, but fell against the bed, sending his backside into a painful spasm.

A friendly, professional smile curved Hannah's luscious lips when she walked in, and Jake clenched his jaw to hide his misery. He must look ridiculous with his pants around his ankles.

"Are you all right?" she asked, indicating his state of undress. "Do you need help?"

He grinned. "Doc, I've never had a woman offer to help me *get* dressed before."

She simply rolled her eyes. "I'll go get a wheelchair."

When she slipped out the door, he chuckled at the blush that had stained her cheeks and kicked off the sweats. Digging in the bag, he found a pair of plain blue plaid cotton boxers from a discount store and pulled them on. They bagged a little on the sides, and he wondered if she'd bought them extra large because of the stitches. Had she bought underwear for her fiancé? Something silky or some of those bikini G-string things?

Several minutes later, Hannah Hartwell appeared at the door with a wheelchair. "Ready to go?"

Jake nodded and limped awkwardly across the room, grateful he could stand. He hated feeling weak and powerless beside her, hated that he had to lean on Hannah to situate himself in the chair. She smiled, handed him a paper bag with his personal items in it, and pushed him through the hallway. Two nurses watched from their station, a tall yuppie-looking doctor eyeing them with interest.

"Since when are you escorting patients out the door, Hannah? Are we short on volunteers or nurses today?"

Hannah's smile seemed strained when she turned to look at him. "No, Seth, this is the man who got shot capturing that thief at my father's car lot. Dad asked me to drive him home."

Jake glanced at the man's name tag. Dr. Seth Broadhurst.

"Can I talk to you for a minute?" Broadhurst asked.

It seemed everyone wanted a word in private with Hannah today.

"Sure." Hannah set the brake on the wheelchair. "Mind if I leave you here for a second, Mr. Tippins?"

Jake shrugged, feeling surly but not knowing the reason. "I'm not going anywhere."

Hannah smiled and took Broadhurst's arm, ushering him into a corner. Jake strained to hear the conversation.

"I've decided to take a little trip, go to that conference in Dallas for a few days, let some of the gossip around here die down.''

''Oh, Seth, I don't want you to go away. If anyone should leave, it should be me.''

Two nurses bustled past, chatting, and a woman dragging a screaming toddler toward the doorway drowned out the rest of the conversation.

Jake noticed Broadhurst squeeze Hannah's hand, lean forward and kiss her on the cheek. A tight sensation gripped Jake's stomach. The man was obviously still in love with Hannah—why else would he have to leave town to recover from their canceled wedding?

Curiosity won over his rational thoughts. When Hannah returned to his side and pushed him into the elevator, he finally asked, ''That one of the surgeons?''

Hannah's blue eyes darkened with anxiety. ''No, he's a psychiatrist.''

''The man you left at the altar?''

Her sharp look told him he'd spoken out of line.

''I didn't dump him, I…'' She stared at the numbers on the elevator as if willing them to signal their arrival at the lobby. ''I don't have to explain my personal relationships to you, Mr. Tippins.''

Jake fisted his hands on his lap. Obviously not. He didn't have to think twice to see the differences between himself and her former fiancé—in her eyes he must look like a low-life salesman, a half-crippled one at that, while Broadhurst was a professional who probably made megabucks. He supposed women thought Broadhurst handsome, if they liked the scrawny, yuppie, clean-cut type. Jake had no idea why the thought irked him so much but it did. ''Right. Sorry to intrude.''

Judging from the tension between her and the shrink, there still might be something between them. When

Broadhurst returned from his trip, Hannah would probably wind up back in his arms, or in some other doctor's, so Jake didn't have to feel too guilty about being with her during the interim.

And with Broadhurst out of town, he'd have the perfect opportunity to cozy up to Hannah.

Chapter Six

Hannah helped Jake settle into the front seat of her Volvo, ignoring the little embarrassed chortle he'd emitted when she'd placed the foam doughnut in the seat. Being a patient definitely humbled a person, and she always made a conscious effort to help her patients maintain their dignity. She also avoided personal relationships with them.

Especially patients who worked with her father.

Why had Wiley been so stubborn earlier? Just because he'd made a good profit this month, he felt he owed her a tidy sum to help pay off her medical-school loans. But Hannah insisted on paying her own way, had never taken money from him and didn't intend to now, at least not for herself. She'd simply put the money in a fund for a graduation party for Alison.

Determined to spend as little time as possible with her father's employee, she maneuvered her car into the light afternoon traffic. "Where do you live, Mr. Tippins?"

"Call me Jake."

Hannah's fingers tightened around the steering wheel at the sound of his husky low voice. Somehow calling him by his first name seemed so…intimate. "All right, Jake. Where can I take you?"

"I'm renting one of those little duplexes on Ivy Street. Do you know where they are?"

"Sure. I'll have you home in a jiffy." *Then I can get away from you.*

"No hurry. I suppose I'll be taking a couple of days off work."

His tone implied he didn't relish the idea of a forced vacation.

"Dad will definitely cover your salary, Jake, plus the hospital bills and any further treatment you need. After all, you were hurt on the job."

"I'm not worried about the money," he said tightly.

Hannah winced. Apparently she'd stepped on that abominable male pride again.

"Sorry, I just wanted you to be able to relax and take it easy."

"Doctor's orders?"

"Yes." Out of the corner of her eye, Hannah caught him staring at her. Masculinity oozed from every pore of the man's big long body. Dark stubble grazed his wide chin, his bronze skin giving him an even darker, more sensual look. His thick blunt fingers were wrapped around the envelope containing his wallet and keys, and his legs were so long they touched the dash. His brawny body and sexy gaze oozed with testosterone. And those eyes, darker than any chocolate she'd ever seen, were tinted with flecks of gold that made her think of snuggling by a fire on a cozy, dark night.

A lazy grin spread on his face as if he recognized the electricity humming between them and planned to stoke the fire. Well, she didn't. She didn't like this…this weird hot feeling that strummed through her body every time he looked at her or simply spoke her name. Her granny had been mistaken about him being her destiny. He was the exact opposite of what she wanted in a man—she wanted calm, safe, someone who didn't rattle her.

"So, with Wiley's connections, why aren't you driving a Porsche or some sporty little convertible?"

"I happen to like my Volvo, Mr. Tippins."

"Jake."

"What?"

"You called me Mr. Tippins again. Mr. sounds too formal, especially considering…"

Heat rushed up Hannah's neck, uncharacteristic of her. Their meeting hadn't been personal, but professional. "All the more reason I should stick to formalities. You're my patient, Mr. Tippins."

"Not anymore. At least not technically." He smiled a warm, sexy smile. "Humor me, then, all right?"

"All right, Jake, but back to my car. I like Volvos. They're safe and dependable." *And boring, like her.*

"You're not a daredevil, huh?"

"Hardly."

"That the reason you decided not to get hitched yesterday?"

No, I cancelled the wedding after I dreamt about you. Hannah bit down on her lip and shot him an impatient look. "I simply decided Seth and I weren't right for each other. We're still friends though."

Judging from their earlier encounter, the man obviously wanted more. "So Broadhurst *is* the daredevil type?"

Hannah chuckled in spite of herself. "No. Seth's even more…conservative than I am."

"Oooh, you started to say boring, didn't you?"

"No."

He was safe, the very reason I wanted to marry him.
Yet, she didn't truly love Seth and she knew that now. She admired his professional manner, even liked him immensely, but love? No.

Perturbed at the way he'd read her mind, Hannah decided to change the subject. "How long have you been working for my father?"

His dark gaze finally pivoted toward the scenery. "Not long. Couple of weeks."

"You like the job?"

Jake's big shoulders lifted slightly. "It's a decent living. Your dad's a pretty interesting guy."

She let that comment slide. "You've sold cars before?"

"No."

"What did you do before you came to Sugar Hill?"

"Oh, a little of this, a little of that." He shaded his eyes with his hand at the blinding sunlight when they turned the street. "I like to move around a lot."

"I see." A vague, short answer. Was he simply a drifter taking odd jobs or was he hiding something? Their conversation died as Hannah turned into the complex of apartments. A few children rode paint-chipped bikes in the street, another group played softball in the cul de sac. Two little girls wearing T-shirts and jeans jumped rope in their driveway. The places looked old, a little unkempt, the grass growing in haphazard patches, as if the owners either didn't care about the appearances or couldn't afford the upkeep.

"I'm in 3B," he said, pointing to a gray wooden structure with a broken-down fence.

She parked the car in the drive and killed the engine. "Just sit tight and I'll come around and help you."

Before she could circle the front, he'd opened the door, grabbed the sides of the car door and lifted himself from the seat. Hannah recognized a man full of pride and placed a tentative hand out to help him.

"I can do it," he said between gritted teeth.

"Look, Mr. Tippins, I'm—"

"Jake."

"Jake, I'm a doctor and you're an injured man. If you fall and reopen your wound, we'll be heading back to the ER."

He nodded tightly, his only concession. Hannah curved her arm around his waist, her breath hitching as he reluctantly draped his arm around her shoulders. For a fraction of a second, his gaze locked with hers. His height dwarfed her, his size and strength almost intimidating. But the sharp flicker of emotion that darted in his eyes scared her far more than his size.

Desire.

Sweet, hot, fiery hunger that sent a ripple of heat soaring through her body. Why hadn't she felt this way when Seth held her?

Hannah sucked in a sharp breath. At the harsh sound, his gaze lowered to her mouth, then to her hand where she gripped his waist. "Am I hurting you?"

He meant was his weight hurting her, she realized, although she instinctively knew that getting involved with him could hurt her much much more. She didn't indulge in one-night stands, illicit affairs or dead-end dates. "No. I'm stronger than I look."

"That a fact?"

"Yes," Hannah whispered, hating the breathy sound of her voice. He smelled of antiseptic and hospital soap and pure male, his solid muscular chest like a wall of granite beneath her hand. His heart beat steadily, pound-

ing with an intensity that spoke of strength and determination. They moved slowly, awkwardly up the steps.
He leaned against her slightly while digging inside the
envelope for the key. When he finally opened the door,
he tried to push away from her, determined to prove he
could stand on his own two feet, but Hannah refused to
release him until they stood beside the couch, a thread-
bare plaid sofa that looked as if it had come straight
from Goodwill.

"I rented the place furnished," he said, as if he read
the questions in her eyes. "It's easier to pick up and
leave that way."

The second time he'd mentioned that he moved
around a lot. His house mirrored the truth of his words.
Three cardboard boxes sat in the small den, the contents
spilling out as if he virtually lived out of them. No
pictures, personal or decorative, adorned the walls or
filled the built-in wooden shelves flanking the gas fireplace. An eerie kind of loneliness echoed off the shabby
bare walls. At the hospital, she remembered Jake saying
he had no family to call and wondered what had happened to them.

She gave herself a mental shake while he angled himself into a semi-comfortable position on the sofa.
Whether or not the man was all alone in the world or
wandered the streets with no job at all shouldn't matter
to her. After all, he made no bones about the fact that
he wasn't a settle-down type of guy so he obviously
didn't miss his family or want one of his own. Definitely not the kind of man Hannah would ever get involved with.

So why the heck had she dreamed about him as if he
were her destiny?

JAKE WATCHED HANNAH fidget with her hands and fought a chuckle. After he'd situated himself on the sofa, she'd made a quick trip to her car and returned with two bags of groceries, then packed them in his cupboards. Not only had the woman bought him clothes and underwear, but now she'd bought him food. A regular little caretaker.

"I'll just heat you some soup, then leave you alone to rest."

"You don't need to—"

"Yes, I do. I promised my father I'd take care of you personally today," she said softly. She leaned against the doorjamb, her luminous blue eyes sparkling in her heart-shaped face.

His gut clenched at the wariness in her expression. And the sweet scent of her delicate skin wafted toward him, reminding him of gardenias. Was it his second, or had it been his third foster mom who'd liked gardenias?

"Dad had to go out of town this morning to film that ad or he would have driven you home himself."

"I know. Wiley told me." He grimaced silently, trying to forget her intoxicating scent and wondering what exactly Wiley was up to in Atlanta. An innocent ad or something more devious—like meeting with potential buyers for his stolen cars? Irritation crawled through him. Wiley's absence from the dealership would have provided the perfect opportunity for Jake to sneak into his office and check out his computer files. Besides, Joey DeLito, Wiley's right-hand man and the person Jake suspected of being the main front man, would be running the place. He could have watched DeLito for signs of subterfuge, maybe even found some concrete evidence to tie up this case so he could move on.

"Jake, are you all right?" The concern in Hannah's

voice startled him. There was nothing personal here—
not with Dr. Hartwell. Hell, Wiley was probably afraid
he'd sue him so he'd sent Hannah to baby-sit. Or maybe
Wiley suspected Jake's real reason for being in Sugar
Hill and wanted Hannah to spy on him.

The mere thought angered him, cementing his resolve
to have her help him.

"I'm fine." He reached for the remote, but she beat
him to it and placed it beside him on the scarred end
table. Their fingers brushed slightly as he took it, and
their gazes locked. He felt a current of something spark
to life between them, reflected both in the way her hand
trembled and the small hitch of her breath. Still, male
pride reared its stubborn head and he heard himself say,
"Look, doc, I know you're a busy lady. If you need to
go back to the hospital, I can take care of myself."

"My shift's over for today. I'm sure you're still tired
from the surgery though, so I'll only stay long enough
to make sure you're fed and tucked in bed."

That image definitely disturbed him. As if she read
his lascivious thoughts, she scurried away to the kitchen
like a doe caught in the headlights of a car. If she intended to spy on him for her dad, she certainly lacked
experience or else she'd probably already be trying to
seduce the truth from him.

From his position on the sofa, he saw her bend over
to search for a pot in his tiny kitchen. Her long black
skirt stretched taut across a firm little backside, rising
slightly to give him an enticing view of her ankles.

Good lord, he was getting turned on by her ankles.

This little plan of his might be more difficult than
he'd imagined.

"I hope you like chicken soup, although I picked up
a can of vegetable and one of clam chowder, or I could

make you a sandwich. I know the hospital food is less than desirable. You probably ate instant pudding and their eggs taste like rubber and—''

''I'm not a picky eater,'' he said, chuckling at the way she rambled on. For some reason, the good doctor seemed nervous as hell around him. Because they were in his apartment alone? It certainly wasn't like he had enough energy to attack her after just being shot. Of course, she might feel weird being near him after her recent breakup with that shrink. Maybe she'd already started plotting a reconciliation.

He flipped on the TV, frowning at the news report. A short clip highlighted news of the attempted robbery, flashing a brief photo of Jake and the subsequent arrest of the punk responsible for the shooting. Finally the reporter switched to international news. Jake prayed his cover wouldn't be blown by the picture.

''The soup's heating.'' She appeared in the doorway again, her slender arms folded across her waist, accentuating the enticing sight of her breasts. ''Can I get you anything else? Ginger ale, a soda, coffee?''

''Maybe some coffee.''

Her shy gaze met his and he felt sucker punched. He wanted to assure her she could relax beside him, that he wouldn't hurt her, but his words would be a lie. Her hesitancy to get near him suggested she wouldn't warm to the idea either. Vulnerability was written all over her delicate features, evident in the way she held herself in the doorway edge, the way she refused to stay still for more than two seconds.

An odd reaction for such a beautiful tempting woman. Or was she simply being coy? Since she'd called off her engagement, she'd have her choice of men pursuing her, all kinds of doctors, other professionals. Distinguished physicians whose salaries were quadruple his. Men who had degrees from Ivy League schools, who drove fancy sports cars, men who had intelligence and brains and the class he'd never have. Yet, as comfortable as she'd been in the ER, her little display of nerves made him want to reach out and comfort her. Tease her until she released those inhibitions and let down her defenses around him. After all, he had to win her trust if she was going to confide the details of Wiley's business....

She disappeared into the kitchen again, gliding back seconds later with a tray laden with soup, crackers, a cup of hot coffee and a slender flower vase holding a single red rose. His eyes narrowed, his stomach knotted. What the...?

"I thought it might cheer you up," Hannah said when his gaze flew to her face.

Nobody had ever given Jake Tippins a flower. He didn't know why the gesture snuck under his skin. Maybe because his own mother hadn't bothered to take care of him when he'd been sick as a child. She'd left him to fend for himself.

"Jake, are you okay?"

He dragged his gaze away from her worried face, and reminded himself she was only doing her job, taking care of him out of some misguided duty to her father who felt he owed Jake. Heck, Wiley might have even funded her medical degree with money he'd earned through illegal means.

"I'm fine." He broke the crackers into the steaming broth, determination replacing any sentiment over Hannah Hartwell. He had to forget the damn rose.

He had a mission. And he couldn't allow her soft vulnerability, no matter how real, to mellow his hardened heart, because if he did break through that barrier between them, any steamy looks she might possibly give him in the future would turn to ice when he locked dear old Wiley in jail.

HANNAH CHUCKLED to herself as she drove home—she'd never met a man more full of male pride than Jake Tippins. Nor one who sent out such mixed messages. When she'd offered to help him to bed, he'd first looked at her with open invitation in his eyes, blatant sexuality and raw hunger so strong that it seemed to flow naturally from the man. But the minute she'd mentioned her father, he'd barked out that she didn't owe him because he'd helped protect Wiley's business. Then she'd asked, as nicely as she knew how, if he wanted her to place the rose by his bed.

Seconds later, he'd become sullen and all but thrown her out of his apartment.

Men—who could figure them out?

The porch light gleamed across her neatly manicured lawn, the tidy pots of pansies adding color and a hominess that welcomed her. They also reminded her of the rundown place where Jake lived. All alone.

Ignoring a twinge of sympathy, she climbed from her car and walked up the stoop, pausing to scoop up her cat, Oreo. The black-and-white feline purred and nestled against her chest as she unlocked the door. Soft light illuminated the entryway, casting golden shadows around the foyer. Hannah smiled at the dozens of photographs framed on the wall. Photos of her family—she and Mimi and Alison growing up, their Dad in some of his silly moments as he entertained them, Grammy Rose.

But no pictures of her mother.

Still, the wall painted a picture of family, of love and good times, things that seemed to be missing from Jake Tippins's life. Compassion welled in her chest and she snuggled Oreo tighter.

"Poor man. He's all alone, kitty. I can see why he's such a grouch. So sad not to have anyone at all." She poured cat food into a bowl, gently placed the feline on his special placemat, then went to the bedroom to undress. All along the way, reminders of her family seemed to jump out at her—the lace doily her grandmother had made, the Tiffany lamp she'd inherited when her other grandmother had passed away, the Victorian settee her parents had bought when they'd first married, the clay vase Mimi had made for her when she was five, the achievement ribbon Alison had had framed after Hannah had encouraged her to take swimming lessons.

And in her bedroom—the hope chest her Grandmother Rose had just sent her.

Flashbacks of her wedding disaster assaulted her. She stared at the beautiful bride doll perched on the chaise beside the hope chest, then walked over and fingered the delicate lace of Grammy Rose's bridal gown. Her gaze fell on her hand where the heirloom ring winked at her in the light from the window.

That crazy dream.

She needed to have her head examined. Determined to end this irrational musing, she decided to make an appointment with a psychiatrist. She'd find someone outside the hospital so she wouldn't feed the hospital grapevine any more than she already had.

Chapter Seven

The next morning, Jake hobbled to the desk in the corner of the bedroom and set up his laptop, logging onto the police search engine to check for an update on the movement of any stolen cars. He scrubbed a hand over his tired eyes, automatically reaching for his coffee and sipping the strong black brew while he waited for the requested information. The chief had given him a deadline, but he hoped to have the case solved way before Christmas and get back to the city.

Early-morning sunlight flickered off the white vase on his nightstand, highlighting dust motes and the faded paint on the walls behind his bed, but his gaze caught the flash of color from the red rose Hannah had brought him, and a strange feeling suffused him.

Why the heck had the simple gesture affected him so?

The sexy doctor's image had filled his dreams, her elusive scent mingling with the sweet hint of the rose fragrance and the raw earthy smell of desire. He'd found himself waking to an empty bed and not liking it.

Shaking off the sensations, he frowned when the doorbell rang, wondering if Wiley had returned from his venture and dropped by with his burly good cheer to thank him again. The man's good-natured bantering had almost severed Jake's last nerve the past two weeks—Wacky Wiley was perpetually happy and boisterous, spreading his exuberance around the car lot and planning another of his outlandish advertising stunts. The man even sang in the morning.

He wondered if Hannah Hartwell did also.

The doorbell rang again, saving him from further torturous musing.

Snapping the screen top to his laptop closed in case Wiley wandered back to his bedroom, Jake slowly rose and hobbled to the door. His stomach growled just as he swung it open.

Hannah Hartwell stood on the stoop, laden with a paper bag full of doughnuts and a smile that held more sunshine than the sun shining in the clear blue sky above.

Damn. Had she been humming?

"I thought I'd drop off some breakfast on my way to the hospital. I noticed your cupboards were pretty bare last night," she said in a rush.

And so was his bed, but he didn't mention that tidbit. "Thanks, Doc, but you don't owe me—"

"I know, but I really didn't mind." Her worried gaze flickered over him. "I'm a doctor, Jake. I simply wanted to make sure you were okay, that you could get around by yourself today."

"I may be slow, but I'm walking," he said.

"Good." She bit down on her lower lip, the sensitive skin puckering red with the nervous gesture. He had a crazy urge to smooth away the tension from her mouth with his tongue, to kiss away the redness. Only he'd nip gently on her lip, then lower….

"I…well, I guess I should go then."

"Did you want to come in?" he asked, kicking himself for forgetting his manners and his plan. He was supposed to try to gain her trust and seduce her into spilling information about her father. Instead, he'd been staring at her sea-blue eyes and silky blond hair like a lust-struck teenager.

"Oh, no, I can't." She gestured toward her dependable Volvo parked in the drive. "I have to get to the hospital. I just wanted to check on you before I started my shift."

It was barely 6:00 a.m. "How long do you work?"

Her eyes crinkled together. "My shift technically ends at three. Why, do you need some help?"

"No, I was just wondering."

"I can come by and bring dinner for you—"

"Dinner sounds good," he said, almost laughing when her eyes widened in shock. She obviously hadn't expected him to agree.

"Well, um, okay." Her professional smile back in place, she reached inside her pocket, pulled out a business card and handed it to him. "Here's the number for the hospital and my beeper number if you need anything."

Then she turned and fled toward her car as if a pack of bloodhounds had picked up her scent and were bearing down on her. Jake watched her drive away, wondering about Hannah. She'd secured her beautiful blond hair in a topknot with only a few loose tendrils curving around her slender face. Her demure manner and conservative clothing certainly couldn't be construed as wanton—except in his wicked mind. Was she the temptress her beauty suggested or the shy, reserved doctor she appeared to be?

Could she possibly know something about her father's business, be involved in the illegal affairs, or was she innocently oblivious to the situation brewing at Wiley's famous used-car lots?

He had to know for sure.

Dinner would be a start. He hobbled back to his laptop, yanked out a creme-filled doughnut and bit into the gooey center, confused. For the first time in his life, he truly hoped one of his suspects turned out to be as innocent as she appeared.

HANNAH STEPPED out of the elevator, inhaling sharply at the frantic sounds around her. For a small-town hospital, they'd had an unusual number of emergencies today. The ER had been a hotbed of chaos since she'd arrived. Probably due to the holiday rush.

And the oddest things had come in today—a little boy with reindeer ears superglued to his head, a toddler who'd stuck a bean seed in her ear weeks ago and had sprouted beans in her ear canal, and a woman who claimed she was missing her invisible dog. Hannah had referred her to the psyche ward.

"Car accident coming in! We'll need a crash cart!"

"Skateboarder with head injury on his way!"

She cringed as she thought about her youngest sister, Alison, and all the daredevil sports she enjoyed. What if…?

No, Alison was fine. Mimi was fine. Her father was fine. Grammy Rose was fine. They would all be together on Thanksgiving.

For some odd reason, Jake's face sprang into her mind.

But Jake Tippins wasn't family.

Sirens wailed and the staff gathered near the entrance, each falling into place as the doors swung open and the

EMTs rushed in. Hannah took a calming breath, summoning strength and locking her emotions into a steel vault, then put Jake Tippins firmly out of her mind.

"SO, HOW ARE you feeling, Tippins?" Wiley asked later that afternoon. He had stopped by on his way back from Atlanta.

"Fine." Jake poured Wiley a bourbon and cola and fixed himself a club soda while Wiley strode across Jake's living room and made himself at home in the comfortable recliner.

He'd been firmly entrenched in the midst of his research when the older man had suddenly appeared at the door. Jake had to keep him from going into his bedroom. One look at the information he'd printed from his computer and Wiley would nail him as an impostor. Jake had tried to get rid of him at the door, but Wiley had bounded in. Dressed in a polyester suit that screamed of the seventies, his thick curly hair slicked away from his forehead with something that smelled faintly like Brylcreem, he stretched out his legs and crossed his ankles as if he planned to stay a while. Something Jake could definitely do without.

His suspicions had instantly mounted.

Wiley could have contacts in Atlanta, could have met with someone today who'd recognized Jake's face from the photo they'd flashed on the news when he'd been shot.

"Not in pain, are you?" Wiley asked, wincing as Jake hobbled across the room.

"No, just a little stiff."

"You know I can't thank you enough for what you did. Although I'd never expect one of my employees to put himself in danger just to save one of our vehicles."

Wiley's voice grew gruff. Either he was a consummate liar or actually sincere, maybe even harboring feelings of guilt.

Jake didn't buy into the act, and Wiley had to be acting. After all, he'd never known a doting father and couldn't imagine one existed. Except Wiley did seem to genuinely care for his daughters. But Wiley barely knew him—why would he be so concerned if he weren't worried about a lawsuit or his illegal activities being exposed?

"I didn't mean to put myself in danger," Jake said, downplaying his instinctual reactions. "I grabbed the kid before I thought."

"You didn't realize he had a gun?"

Jake shrugged. "He was only a kid. I figured I could move faster than him." He indicated his lopsided walk with a self-deprecating laugh. "Guess I'm not as young as I used to be."

Wiley laughed good-naturedly, then sipped his drink while Jake tried to sit down. Getting comfortable took a while, and the awkward silence in the interim gave Jake time to study Wiley. Minutes earlier, he'd discovered a group of Hondas missing from south Georgia. Thirteen reported stolen in one month—he'd have to be on the lookout for them to come rolling through the dealership. Of course, they'd be painted, new tag numbers issued, and Wiley wouldn't be so stupid as to allow more than one to surface at a time.

"So, how did the taping go?" Jake asked.

"Went pretty good, son, except the turkey wouldn't cooperate. Dumb bird kept getting its feathers all in a titter right when I jumped in with my line."

"A real turkey?" Jake asked, wondering at Wiley's common sense when it came to publicity. Still, maybe his riotous ads were a front for his highly skilled illegal operations. If he appeared to be a harebrained comic, no one would suspect him of being the mastermind of a statewide crime ring.

"Yeah, we had a couple of big gobblers just to add some authenticity. Then one of the salesgirls dressed up in a turkey suit." Wiley rubbed his hands across his thighs and laughed. "Wouldn't mind having a little of that bird myself for Thanksgiving dinner, if you know what I mean."

Jake forced a grin at the glib comment. Wiley seemed to enjoy women although he hadn't actually noticed anyone special in the man's life.

"I arranged to have one of my finest dropped off for you to drive around, just as a thank-you," Wiley said.

"I have my Jeep, Wiley."

"I know, but you can give it a rest. Do some advertising for me. It's a vintage silver El Camino convertible. Just got her in."

Nothing conspicuous.

"That is, unless you'd rather drive the pink Cadillac—"

"No, that's fine." Jake's hand tightened around his glass. "But lending me a car isn't necessary."

Wiley raised his hand to silence him. "Please accept the gesture. You're a hero, you should drive something showy." A sheepish grin tilted the corner of his mouth. "I also arranged to have some food delivered, to tide you over till you're ready to go out."

Jake *was* ready to go out, but didn't comment. He hated being cooped up in the house and much preferred wide-open spaces to confinement. Another product of his upbringing.

Wiley stood and polished off his drink. "Anything

else you need, you just let me know.'' He offered his hand for a handshake and Jake accepted it, unable to grasp the real Wiley Hartwell. One minute the man acted like a raucous fool, planning outlandish publicity stunts and dressing his sales staff up like birds and elves, the next minute he appeared to be a genuine friend and an overly concerned parent.

''Call me if you need anything, son.'' A motor rumbled outside and Wiley darted to the window, his boisterous voice full of enthusiasm. ''There's the truck of food now.''

Jake stood in silence as two men began to unload bags of groceries from a white van and haul them into his house. As he watched, Joey DeLito, Wiley's right-hand man, drove up in the shiny silver El Camino.

A thought suddenly hit him. If Wiley had discovered Jake's true identity, perhaps this little car wasn't exactly a payback for his heroics, but a bribe.

All the more reason he should cozy up to Wiley's darling daughter.

Chapter Eight

"So, Dr. Hartwell, you have something on your mind?" Dr. Edwin McCoy, a specialist in dream analysis, angled his lean body into his leather chair, propped a gold pen against his notepad, ready to listen.

Hannah's stomach lurched. Earlier, it had seemed like a good idea to consult a psychiatrist about the dream—now she simply felt foolish.

She gripped the chair and started to stand. "I-I'm not sure I need to be here."

One dark brow arched. "Which probably is a good indicator that you do."

Hannah paused, struggled to control her panic, then finally forced herself to relax on the plush love seat facing him. She absolutely drew the line at lying down.

"Why don't you tell me what's on your mind?" Dr. McCoy began. "Stress with the job? Personal problems?"

Although McCoy didn't work at Sugar Hill with Seth, they were acquaintances.

He obviously knew about her canceled wedding. Was he defensive for Seth? "Maybe this isn't a good idea. I know you and Seth are friends."

"Professional acquaintances, Dr. Hartwell. That's all. Everything you tell me will be held in confidence."

Meaning he wouldn't tell everyone she was having psychotic thoughts. Relief should have spilled through her at the thought, but her stomach quivered too much for her to relax.

The doctor put his pen aside, folded his hands and leaned forward. "Hannah, I can't help you if you don't talk to me. Now please tell me what's bothering you."

His mild tone and less formal posture helped to put her at ease. Oh, well, she might as well share her odd situation and find out if she was a candidate for the loony farm.

"It's not work," she said slowly.

"Personal then?"

Hannah nodded. "You see I have this kooky grandmother..."

Thirty minutes later, she finished and leaned back against the love seat, exhausted. "I need to know if I'm losing my mind."

"You say there's no history of psychic tendencies in your family?"

"Not that I'm aware of. But I don't believe in folktales...it's like believing in magic."

A small smile curved his mouth. "You don't believe in magic?"

"No, do you?"

He chuckled. "It doesn't matter what I believe. We're talking about you."

"But do you think there can be any truth to that silly legend?"

"I don't know. I do think magic exists between people though. Most of the time it's referred to as chemistry."

"A simple physical response," Hannah concluded. "I've read all about pheromones."

The doctor steepled his fingers, studying her. "Did you believe in magic when you were a child?"

"Well, yes."

"You say that with hesitancy."

"Everyone grows up, Dr. McCoy."

"Is there some other reason you stopped believing? Some incident that forced you to grow up quickly?"

Hannah chewed her lip. "I suppose the day my mother left could account for my feelings, but I got over that a long time ago. What does it have to do with the present?"

"A parent's desertion can have devastating results, Hannah," he said in a low tone. "Sometimes we think we've dealt with those feelings, but we've only suppressed them."

"I told you this has nothing to do with my mother leaving," Hannah argued. "I simply want to understand why I dreamt about a strange man with whom I have absolutely nothing in common."

"Are you attracted to the man?"

Hannah twisted the cuff of her blouse, avoiding eye contact. "Well, yes…I mean physically." Her gaze swung to his. "But that's all. He's totally wrong for me."

"Are you sure?"

"Are you sure you don't want to show me some ink blots and let me analyze them?"

Dr. McCoy chuckled. "No. I think talking is much more helpful."

Yeah, because it wasn't him spilling his guts and soul. She jiggled her foot, tapping it against the chair edge. "Can't you just hook me up to some electrodes and see if my brain's functioning okay?"

"I don't think that's necessary. And I don't think you're losing your mind."

"You think it might be an early hormonal thing? Premature menopause?"

A grin tugged at the corner of his mouth. "Hannah, you're only in your twenties."

"Maybe I have a chemical imbalance, some—"

"Hannah, I don't believe your dream is a symptom of a serious illness."

Frustration filled her. "Then why would I have an erotic dream about a stranger?"

His mouth twisted sideways as he contemplated her question. "There could be several reasons. Whether you want to admit it or not, working in the ER is definitely stressful. You deal with life-and-death situations and sometimes only have seconds to react." His voice held a note of compassion. "You have to be affected when you lose a patient. Maybe you should talk to a friend, unwind when things happen."

"I don't like to burden people," Hannah said. "I can handle the stress of my job."

He nodded, although Hannah sensed he didn't quite believe her. "There could be other factors, too. Knowing your parents' marriage didn't work out might have played on your subconscious, making you panic about your own upcoming nuptials."

Thank God he'd said something that made sense. *Stress.* Her whole dream had been a reaction to a build-up of stress.

"Maybe you're confused about what you really want in a relationship. Most specifically in a man."

"I know exactly what I want. Someone dependable, intelligent, settled—"

The doctor's eyebrows rose again. "Perhaps those are qualities you think you want. But on a deeper level, you want more. You probably saw this man somewhere, found him attractive, and his image triggered other qualities that sparked your interest. Maybe you should get to know him and see if you two hit it off."

"Because…?"

"You felt a certain chemistry with him that you hadn't experienced before. My guess is the feeling was new and answered a deeper need. He may or may not be a suitable partner, but he represents excitement, taking a risk, all those things you're afraid of."

"I'm not afraid of excitement," Hannah argued, wincing at the petulant edge in her voice.

"Maybe not. But, considering the fact that your mother left you, it's understandable you might be afraid of getting too close to someone for fear of abandonment and getting hurt again."

Hannah stared at him, annoyed when tears suddenly moistened her eyes. Her throat thick with emotion, she stood and thanked him for his time. He was wrong, she told herself as she left his office. She was not afraid to love someone. She'd dealt with her mother's desertion a long time ago. And she didn't intend to dwell on her lost childhood or her parents' divorce.

No, his first comment had hit the nail on the head. Her work in the ER created stress. She was simply reacting to being on overload. On her way home, she'd stop and buy one of those books on some kind of meditation, or buy some health-food supplement to help her moods. Or maybe she'd take up exercising. She'd jog until she dropped from exhaustion, until she could sleep without having any more weird dreams. Then her life would return to normal.

LATER THAT EVENING, Hannah pulled into Jake's drive, exhausted, but determined to carry through on her promise to check on her father's employee. She'd stopped and bought a book on relaxation techniques and dream analysis, then picked up Italian food for dinner. She intended to drop off the meal, retreat to her own place, take a nice long bubble bath and crash. The only positive thing about having such a hectic, nonstop afternoon—she hadn't had time to think about Jake Tippins. Well, not much anyway.

With a weary sigh, she dragged herself from her car, her gaze resting on the classic convertible parked by Jake's rusted-out SUV. No doubt her father had dropped the vintage car off for Jake to drive. She wondered what the big, proud Mr. Tippins thought about her father's kind gesture.

Feeling calmer, she raised her hand and knocked on the door. Seconds ticked by while she tapped her foot up and down on the cement step, trying to be patient. The poor man had been shot, it wasn't actually easy for him to get up and down or walk around. She knocked again.

The door swung open and she blinked in astonishment. He appeared in the doorway, wearing a dark maroon T-shirt that hugged his muscular arms and broad shoulders and emphasized his tanned complexion. A pair of loose-fitting jeans hung low on his lean hips, also drawing attention to his incredible male physique. From his musky scent, she realized he'd showered and obviously shaved, even tried to comb the overly long strands of his dark hair into a fashionable style. But he still looked like some renegade who should be driving a motorbike.

"Hi."

His dark gaze raked over her, lingering momentarily on her disheveled appearance, and came to rest on her eyes. "You look tired. Bad day?"

"We had a lot of emergencies. How are you feeling?"

"I wish everyone would stop asking me that."

Hannah arched an eyebrow. "Everyone?"

"You. Your dad."

"I see he dropped by bearing gifts." Hannah nodded toward the plush convertible.

Jake's tight smile didn't surprise her. He obviously didn't like to owe anyone. "Yeah. Said it would be good advertising." He opened the door wider. "You want to come in?"

"No, thanks, I'm really tired. I'm going home—"

"Wiley tried to call you around five but they said you'd already left the ER."

The paper bag of food crinkled in Hannah's hands. She'd been in Dr. McCoy's office, but she didn't want to tell anyone she'd seen a psychiatrist. Fumbling for an excuse, she tapped her fingers along the bag. "I...had some errands to do. Laundry, drop off some videos, I needed to stop by the drugstore...." She realized she was rambling and closed her mouth, aware his dark eyes studied her intently.

"Have you already eaten?" Jake asked.

"No, but I'll fix something at home."

"That's ridiculous." He indicated the hefty bag she carried. "Whatever you have in there smells delicious, and it looks as if you brought enough for an army."

Remembering her conversation with the psychiatrist,

she thought she should relent, suffer through the meal and prove to herself that Jake Tippins did not affect her. But she was simply too exhausted to deal with the man. "You can have leftovers tomorrow. I really have to go."

"All work and no play makes for a dull life," he said, teasing.

Her lips tightened into a thin line. "I like my life just fine. Besides I do have work to do." *And I'm going home, run a few miles, take a bath and forget about you.*

Without another word, she turned and headed to her car. She wasn't afraid, she told herself, as she drove away. She simply needed a good night's sleep, free from dreams of Jake Tippins.

Jake tried to ignore the sting of rejection that accompanied Hannah's refusal to have dinner with him as he unloaded the bag and served himself a plate of the steaming lasagna, but her attitude irked. Did she really have work to do, or was she simply using her job as an excuse to avoid spending time with him? Was his company so distasteful to her that she couldn't manage a meal with him? Granted he wasn't a doctor or a shrink like her former boyfriend, and he didn't have a degree, but...

He refused to compare himself to Broadhurst. After all, it wasn't like he was *really* interested in dating Hannah—this was just work.

He thought about her odd reaction when he'd mentioned Wiley's phone call. She'd tapped her fingers up and down, indicating nerves. He'd bet anything she'd been lying. But why would she lie?

The answer hit him swiftly, jarring him back to his senses. Wily had been anxious to talk to Hannah earlier, had even seemed frazzled when he couldn't locate her—maybe it had something to do with the car ring.

Chapter Nine

"Come on." Mimi tugged Hannah's hand and dragged her off the sofa.

"I'm not in the mood to go by Dad's car lot," Hannah said.

Mimi paused and planted her hands on her hips. "Why not?"

Because Jake will be there.

Even three days after the dream, Hannah still felt a knot in her stomach every time she thought of the man. "I'm not in the holiday mood yet."

Mimi cut off her protests with a wave, flashing her new nail polish—a fluorescent pink she called *I'm Not Really a Waitress.* "It'll be fun, you know Dad always decorates the car lot for Christmas the day before Thanksgiving. Maybe you can help string some lights. I'm going to help Joey hang bows on the glass windows and mistletoe over the entryway, get people in a lovey-dovey mood."

So they would kiss.

She wondered how Jake's mouth would taste, if his kisses would be as hot and dark as his eyes.

"I think Dad bought an eight-foot Santa to perch on the back of one of the convertibles. He's going to decorate it like Santa's sleigh. He even talked about trying to find some real reindeer this year for the Christmas commercial.''

Every year their father's Christmas ads grew more elaborate and inventive. Hannah had once thought all the antics funny, but her mother's abandonment had fast launched her into adulthood. Too bad it hadn't jolted her father into a more mature form of advertising.

''I think he's going to hire some teenage girls to dress up like elves and give out candy, too. Should be fun to watch.''

''That'll certainly draw a crowd,'' Hannah admitted.

''Come on.'' Mimi motioned toward the door.

''Dad doesn't need me,'' Hannah argued. ''The salesmen can help him.'' Although Jake shouldn't be climbing ladders with his injury, she thought with a twinge of worry.

''The salesmen will probably be swamped with all those early-bird specials Dad advertised,'' Mimi said. ''Now, let's move, Hanny. I won't take no for an answer.''

Hannah laughed at the silly childhood name. When she'd lapsed into her too-serious, philosophical, analytical shell, Mimi had always been able to coax a smile from her. Had she really been so serious about life that she'd forgotten how to have fun, even how to enjoy the holiday spirit?

Was she *afraid?*

Her sister wagged a finger at her, indicating her disheveled appearance. ''You've been working yourself day and night ever since you called off your wedding to Seth. What are you trying to do, punish yourself?''

Hannah winced at how close her sister had come to the truth. She had thought she should somehow make up for being irresponsible by helping out more in the ER. And work was the only thing that kept her from obsessing over that crazy dream and this totally insane attraction to Jake Tippins.

Of course, maybe he wouldn't be at the dealership. Or maybe he'd be so busy selling cars he wouldn't even notice her. And maybe when she saw him this time, her reaction would be rational, sane, dispassionate.

"I'm not letting you stay here like some monk anymore." Mimi grabbed her arm and jerked her forward. "It's time you lightened up and had some fun."

"Then we should go someplace besides Dad's car lot."

"Okay, how about a strip club?"

"Mimi, can't you think of anything besides sex?"

Mimi's smile faded into bewilderment. "Well, you're the Scrooge who doesn't want to help us decorate for Christmas."

"I'm sorry," Hannah said, well aware Mimi had good intentions.

"I told you I won't let you sit here and pine anymore."

"I'm not pining."

"Strip club or Dad's?"

"How about a *movie*." Hannah tried to extract herself from Mimi's catlike clutches, but Mimi dragged her through the door and hauled her up the sidewalk.

"Look, Hannah, Dad's worried about you and—"

"Tell Dad not to worry. I can take care of myself."

Mimi huffed, lifting her curly bangs from her forehead as she paused at her car. "You are so damn independent. If you won't go for yourself, at least do it for me. You know the whole family gets together to decorate. It's tradition."

And tradition was important to Mimi. "But Alison won't be there."

"Yes, she will. She came home this morning."

A sharp pain hit Hannah for her selfishness. As fun-loving and erratic as Mimi seemed, she harbored a sentimental side. She'd always insisted on family gatherings for special occasions—probably to make up for their missing mother.

Mimi pointed to her little red sports car. "Now get in or I'm going to phone Dad—"

"All right, I'm coming." Hannah climbed in the car, forcing thoughts of her own life on hold as she contemplated Mimi's cropped top and the expanse of smooth stomach the tiny garment revealed. "So, how are you and Joey getting along?"

Mimi sprinted to the driver's seat, flashing her long legs as she slipped onto the cushy leather. "Okay, but he's been acting a little strange lately. Working day and night."

Hannah buckled her seat belt, bracing herself as Mimi streaked from the driveway, peeling rubber. "It *is* a busy time of year. Maybe he's saving to buy you a nice present for Christmas."

Mimi brightened at the possibility and revved up the engine. "Maybe I'll have to show him this belly-dancing costume I want. I need it to rehearse for a part I'm auditioning for. Did you know they're going to be filming a new soap in Atlanta?"

Hannah rolled her eyes. "No, I didn't know."

"Yeah, it's called *Scandalous*. Anyway, I have a present for Joey tonight. I'm going to surprise him with some whipped cream and strawberries."

''They do say that the way to a man's heart is through his stomach.''

Mimi laughed. ''You're so old-fashioned, sis. There are other ways to a man's heart. Just use your imagination.''

Hannah bit down on her lip and stifled a comeback. She did have an imagination. In fact, her fantasies had caused major problems lately—but unfortunately all her dreams had to do with the sexy man who worked for her dad.

Realizing she'd allowed her mind to wander again, she closed her eyes, trying to remember some of the relaxation techniques from the book. Problem was, so far none of them had worked. She thought of the advice her college speech teacher had given her—*before speaking in front of a group or before an interview, calm your nerves by picturing whoever you're talking to in their underwear.*

Only, Jake in his underwear was the last image she needed in her mind—and it did nothing to calm her nerves.

JAKE SPOTTED two of Wiley's daughters arriving in Mimi's little red sports car and gulped. While Mimi definitely exuded sex appeal with that mass of curly burnt-copper hair and mile-long legs, something about her quiet, subdued sister crawled inside him and twisted every male nerve ending in his body. A deeper kind of innate beauty that wasn't boisterous or showy radiated from Hannah's delicate frame. He could almost see that honey-colored hair fanned out across his pillow, could almost feel the soft pressure of her rose-tipped lips as she allowed him to sip at her mouth….

"Young man, are you listening to me?" Leopard-skin-clad and statuesque, Berta Simpson held out a pudgy hand and tried to stuff a fifty-dollar bill in his hand. "You know I've been eyeing this little baby all week. I have to have her today. Now, let's make a deal."

Jake tried to ignore Hannah as she emerged from the sports car, and forced himself to focus on his customer. Thankfully he didn't have to make a living selling cars or he'd be homeless. He definitely didn't have the charisma Wiley possessed.

"I'm sorry, Mrs. Simpson, but I can't accept a bribe—tip for helping you. I've given you Wiley's bottom price." Annoyance etched itself on her chubby face. He didn't want to cheat the lady, but a fifty-dollar tip wouldn't cut the mustard with his boss if Wiley discovered Jake had shaved another ten thousand off the price. Some people wanted everything for nothing.

He simply wanted to solve this case and get the hell out of Sugar Hill. Too much hominess, small-town life, *family* stuff to suit his tastes. He needed to be back in the city where he could lose himself in the anonymity of the crowd.

Buster, one of Wiley's other salesmen, pulled the gate shut. Although normally they remained opened until nine, Wiley had decided on a six o'clock closing due to Thanksgiving the next day. Another commercialized holiday, Jake thought sourly.

Wiley wandered out of the cement-and-glass building which housed the offices, waving at his daughters. Mimi threw her arms around her father, waving exuberantly toward Joey DeLito. Wiley's right-hand man had settled himself inside to indulge his coffee and chocolate-bar fetish while he wrote up the five sales he'd made that day. Jake had observed him from a distance all day, cataloguing every movement Joey made. He intended to follow up on Joey's record sales by running a check on all of DeLito's customers. He'd managed to use his miniature camera and had taken snapshots of each one. As soon as he could, he'd compare them to every criminal in the police database.

Oddly, Hannah didn't rush to hug her father. The two of them spoke with a slight hesitancy between them just as they had at the hospital. Strange—what was going on between Hannah and Wiley?

Not that he cared personally, he told himself. But if they'd had a rift or if tension existed between them, their awkwardness might have something to do with the case.

Berta exhaled noisily as if she realized she'd lost his attention. "I guess I'll just have to talk to Wiley myself." With a shake of her head reminiscent of a mother hen with her feathers ruffled, she turned and stalked toward the office, her leopard-print purse banging her ripe hips as she strutted. Jake averted his thoughts—she reminded him of turkey on Wiley's latest TV commercial. Jake had seen the early-bird special ad at breakfast and nearly choked on his coffee. So far, the commercial had worked though—the dealership had been swamped all morning with early Christmas shoppers hoping to save a buck. As clumsy with his sales technique as a rookie with a Glock, Jake had actually managed to sell two cars in spite of himself.

Berta launched herself at Wiley and Hannah glanced at him, her blue-eyed gaze wary but full of something else—desire. Unwanted, even hooded, but he definitely saw the spark of sexual arousal in those vibrant blue eyes.

Wiley suddenly wove an arm around Berta's ample frame, whispering something that made the woman blush. Wiley certainly did know how to schmooze. Within seconds, Berta hurried inside the glass-enclosed offices, obviously ready to make a deal. He heard Wiley agree to meet her shortly and realized he'd been staring at Hannah. The fading sunlight dappled her hair and face with a soft glow, the darkening sky creating sultry shadows around her feminine curves.

Not wanting Wiley to guess his intentions toward his oldest daughter, he scanned the parking lot for another customer but remembered they'd closed the lot. Determined to overhear if Wiley and Hannah discussed business, he spotted the string of Christmas lights Wiley wanted around the building, grabbed the ladder, climbed to the top and began to drape the colorful lights.

Mimi sauntered inside to meet Joey. Through the front glass, Jake saw her plant a lip-lock on his mouth.

"Jake, look who's here!" Wiley yelled, ushering Hannah toward him.

Jake stuck his finger with a tack and yelped.

"Are you all right?" Hannah asked.

Why was he forever getting hurt around this woman?

"Fine."

"I'm not sure you should be up there, Mr. Tippins, not with your injury."

So, she'd reverted to Mr. Tippins again?

He shot her a sexy grin meant to rattle her. Although, when her lips parted slightly, his own breath hitched. He tried to steady himself by inhaling, almost lost his balance and nearly toppled off the ladder. His legs swung wildly, his hands gripping the metal rungs in a deathgrip.

Hannah and Wiley grabbed the ladder just in time to save him from falling on his face.

"See what I mean," Hannah said in that irritating professional voice.

The streetlight flickered on, illuminating her golden hair; his gaze was drawn to her rosy mouth. Her father cleared his throat, and Jake realized Wiley was watching him with an odd look in his eyes. Did he know Jake's true identity, or did he suspect Jake's growing interest in his oldest daughter?

"I think I can handle hanging a few Christmas lights, Doc," Jake said. Actually there were *hundreds* of lights. "On your way to the hospital?"

"I've already pulled my shift." Hannah's gaze tracked the enormous tangled vine of lights.

"Decorating this place is a big job," Wiley said in a booming voice. "But it's your lucky day, here, Tippins. My daughters dropped by to help."

Hannah's smile melted into a frown. "Actually, Dad, I—"

"No, baby, this is perfect," Wiley said, releasing his grip on the ladder. "Decorating for the holidays is a family affair with the Hartwells, right, Hannah?"

Hannah nodded tightly.

"You just stand here and help Jake. Alison's hanging bows on all the windows. I'll enlist Joey and Mimi to set up the sleigh exhibit while I talk to Berta."

Wiley ambled off, his jovial smile indicating his excitement over the family project. Jake suddenly felt like an outsider. Family affairs had never been his forte.

Then again, he was only doing a job here. He hadn't been invited to join the family, simply to hang some stupid Christmas lights. He'd take advantage of the opportunity to watch Hannah and Mimi with their father.

Chapter Ten

Hannah averted her gaze from Jake, the height of the ladder putting him at an awkward level; she either had to crane her neck to see his face or stare straight at his backside, which was definitely a mistake. His muscular physique was emphasized by the way the fabric of his khaki slacks stretched taut across his body, and it did strange things to her insides.

"Hold that end for me," Jake said, as Christmas music suddenly began to blare through the speakers. The cheery lyrics of *I Saw Mommy Kissing Santa Claus* did nothing to alleviate the tension thrumming between the two of them. The song reminded Hannah of her missing mother and her childish dreams of having her parents back together.

What was wrong with her? She'd never been sentimental or dwelled on the past.

Obviously that psychiatrist had planted the seed about her parents' divorce in her mind. Now she'd have to figure out how to exorcise it just as she'd tried to do to the dream.

Brushing aside the painful memories, Hannah grabbed the long cord, untangling the winding mass with shaky fingers. Jake looked almost as uncomfortable as she felt. Hadn't he ever strung Christmas lights before, or did he think she'd come here to see him?

"I want you to know I didn't plan to do this today," Hannah said.

He draped a cord over the front entrance. "I thought your dad said you guys always decorate together."

"Mimi likes to but I...well, I thought I'd let them handle it this year."

"Avoiding me, Hannah?"

The softly spoken question took her by surprise. A faint breeze stirred, bringing with it a whiff of his masculine scent. Hannah silently groaned and squinted through the light from the streetlamp to see him staring at her. His blatant look of sexual interest seared through her, heating her already warm face. "No."

"Then you're just a Scrooge, huh?"

Her temper bristled. "No, as a matter of fact, I intend to help decorate the tree in the ER tomorrow."

"Then you like this kind of stuff?"

Hannah shrugged. "Mimi gets into the festivities more than me."

"She is pretty enthusiastic," Jake agreed. "But you look like the picture of gloom. What's wrong, Doc?"

"Nothing." Hannah glanced at the doorway and spotted Mimi and Joey kissing under a sprig of mistletoe. A moment of envy stirred within Hannah at Mimi's innocent enthusiasm. Mimi seemed more Jake's type. So why was Jake interested in her?

"Maybe we should get in the swing of it the way they are," Jake suggested.

Hannah's gaze locked with his, the heat crackling between them. Did he mean they should be kissing like Mimi and Joey?

A half-cocky grin slid onto his face. "What do you say?"

The faint hint of challenge in his voice resurrected the competitive nature she'd normally reserved for school. She'd been determined to make good grades and win respect, hoping to overcome being the butt of the other kids' jokes. Deciding to beat him at his own game and prove to herself she wasn't afraid, Hannah dropped the lights and retrieved another ladder, setting it up a few feet away. "All right, let's light up this place. We'll show them who has the most Christmas spirit."

Jake grinned as if he knew she'd purposely avoided his innuendo.

A tingle of anticipation rippled up her spine at the promise of retribution in his eyes. There was something deeply alluring, albeit troubling, about her father's newest employee. The drifter man could give her a great tumble between the sheets if she simply surrendered to the heat simmering between them, and she could barely resist his sexy smile and teasing overtures.

But she had to resist him. Hannah always did what she should—well, except for not marrying Seth. She'd be absolutely crazy if she succumbed to temptation with Jake Tippins. He'd probably climb out of bed afterwards and skip town before the sheets even grew cold.

And when Hannah took a man to her bed, she intended him to stay there forever.

TWO HOURS LATER, Hannah and Jake had finished stringing the lights. Hannah laughed as they jogged from car to car, attaching big red bows to the hoods. Mimi handpainted signs for the special red-ribbon sales with glittery red paint while Alison sprayed white snow on all the windows surrounding the offices and arranged glow-in-the-dark gold stars in clusters to form the shape of a larger Christmas star on the front door. Wiley had Joey busy rigging a bright red Mustang convertible into a sleigh with a carpet of artificial grass to simulate the lawn.

Wiley plugged in the Christmas lights, illuminating the car lot with twinkling colors, the frame of the building outlined in dozens of bright red and green lights that blinked intermittently, seemingly in tune with the litany of Christmas songs piped over the speakers. As Jake stuck the last bow on a '98 Fiat, he leaned against the car and folded his arms, his gaze traveling over the business establishment with a rueful shake of his head.

"I don't think I've ever seen anything quite like this."

Hannah saw the laughter bubbling in his eyes and couldn't contain her own amusement. "Dad always likes to do things up in a big way."

"It *is* colorful."

"That it is," Hannah admitted with a laugh. "He might win the Tacky Light Show this year."

"I bet families will drive by just to let the kids see the lights. Probably cause a traffic jam."

Hannah smiled, imagining the array of colors through a child's eyes. Young children would be enthralled. But when they grew older and the magic died, they would see her father's overexuberance in a different light—the way the older kids had when they'd teased her.

"I suppose he's going to dress like Santa Claus and let the kids sit in his lap for pictures," Jake said.

"He does every year."

"Does he hire an Easter bunny for Easter?"

"Yeah. He even has an egg hunt in the car lot with

special discounts hidden inside the prize eggs. Oh, and he hides candy for the kids.''

Jake nodded, thinking the man might be flamboyant, but he certainly appeared family-oriented. He also had tapped into some unique marketing strategies which seemed to be working. His smile faded as the real reason he'd come to Sugar Hill rushed back—had Wiley tapped into illegal business dealings as well?

Mimi and Alison's laughter echoed from the front door of the office as they scrutinized Alison's artwork. He glanced up and saw laughter sparkling in Hannah's eyes, and a tug of some emotion he didn't recognize rose inside him. Earlier, Hannah had seemed distracted, even a little sad when she'd first begun helping him string the lights. Did the holidays make her melancholy or was she worried about Wiley, afraid he'd get caught?

He'd been amazed at the good-natured ribbing the three sisters had indulged in while they divvied up the tasks. Teasing and laughter—not the screaming fights he remembered from his own youth. This oddball family worked together well and seemed to have fun doing it. Wiley had even commented that if Hannah hadn't taken up medicine, he'd have handed her the business when he retired.

His throat grew dry when he glanced into Hannah's mesmerizing blue eyes, the sparkle of emotion in the depths twisting something deep inside him. He would destroy this family if he discovered Wiley was making his money through illegal means. And Hannah would never look at him the same way again.

Hannah brushed a strand of hair behind her ear, aware Jake was watching the movement, the vein in his neck throbbing as he swallowed. His neck was long and thick, tapering into shoulders that were so broad they made her feel tiny. Why had she never noticed how sexy a man's throat could be? Or how the simple act of swallowing could be so erotic?

Laughter shrieked behind her and she clenched her hands by her sides and forced herself to remember that she and Jake weren't alone, they were in a public place with her family surrounding them. Thank heavens. Joey and her father conferred in the parking lot, admiring the hundreds of sparkling lights, trying to decide if they needed another row along the sign announcing the name of Wiley's establishment.

"Look, you two, you're standing under the mistletoe," Alison said with a grin.

Hannah and Jake both looked up to see Alison hanging a fresh twig of the greenery above them in the doorway.

"Go on, you have to kiss him, Hannah," Alison said.

"Yeah, kiss him," Mimi yelled.

Heat crept up Hannah's neck, but she turned and saw the flicker of desire and mischief in Jake's eyes and couldn't resist. She slid her hand behind his head, stood on tiptoe and kissed him. His lips were gentle, tentative, but grew firm as he deepened the kiss, the spark of hunger igniting in her body stunning her. When she finally pulled away, Mimi and Alison were both watching with grins on their faces. She tried to steady her breathing, while Jake simply studied her with a dark desire that sent fire rippling through her.

Wiley sauntered over and slapped Jake on the back. "I'd say things look pretty darned good," Wiley boomed. "I think you earned yourself a turkey dinner with us tomorrow, son."

Jake's shocked expression would have been laughable if Hannah hadn't felt panic swelling in her own chest. Her father never invited his salesmen to Thanksgiving dinner—he usually reserved the day for the girls. Even Mimi's boyfriend Joey hadn't been invited. Had Wiley seen the heated kiss?

No, her father wouldn't approve of her and Jake—would he?

"Thanks, Wiley," Jake said, snapping Hannah back to reality. "I appreciate the offer, but I wouldn't want to impose on family. I still have plenty of that food you sent over."

Hannah heard an odd gruffness to his voice and wondered at the reason.

"Nonsense, boy. You got yourself shot trying to guard my business, and you admitted you don't have any family to speak of. We can't let you stay home by yourself all day, now can we, Hannah?"

Hannah hugged her arms around her middle. "Dad, don't be so persistent. Jake may have other plans."

Jake quirked a brow sideways as if he realized she didn't want her father inviting him.

Wiley's green eyes shot toward Jake, a bushy eyebrow arched. "Do you have plans, son? Got a lady friend on the side?"

Jake's jaw tightened, his gaze riveted on Hannah. "Well…no. But I certainly don't mind spending the day alone. I can come over and do some stuff around here if you'd like—"

The frown on Wiley's face stopped Jake in his tracks. "Ain't no employee of mine working on Thanksgiving. Now come on over in the morning. We'll eat our fill and watch football on the tube all day. DeLito's going to come, too. We'll have us some male bonding time."

Joey was coming? Male bonding time? Maybe her craziness was rubbing off on her father?

"All right," Jake agreed.

"The girls will gather early for coffee, and I'll smoke a turkey in the smoker," Wiley said. "Mimi will bring dessert. Hannah always brings these homemade rolls she makes. They just melt in your mouth, son. Alison will throw together some veggies from the freezer. You just bring yourself."

Hannah bit down on her lip—she never made home-made rolls. In fact, the last time she'd tried, she'd burned them so badly that smoke had filled the house, the smoke detector had gone off and the fire department had arrived and ruined the rest of the dinner when they'd opened the water hoses.

"See you about noon." Her father winked at her, then walked back toward the building where Mimi and Joey and Alison stood, adjusting the final touches to the entryway. Snow flurries began to drift from the sky, the whistle of winter biting in the air. Jake Tippins shoved his hands in his pockets with a frown. He looked as if he'd been cornered and didn't know how to extricate himself. If Hannah didn't know better, she'd think her father was actually trying to play matchmaker—to set her up with his newest salesman.

Ridiculous.

Thanksgiving dinner was definitely not conducive to romantic notions. And Wiley simply felt compelled to pay off a debt.

A sigh of relief escaped her. With her family surrounding them, they wouldn't be alone for a single second. She'd be safe. Safe from temptation. Safe from the big man's irresistible sexual draw. And safe from wanting his hot, wild kisses.

Now, she had to go home and learn how to make homemade rolls before noon tomorrow so she wouldn't look like a fool when she showed up empty-handed. And just as soon as she had the chance, she'd sit her father down and find out why he'd told such a ridiculous lie about her.

AS SOON AS Jake left the car lot, he rushed to get the photos developed, then accessed the police database to cross-check for possible connections. Knowing the search would take a while, he fixed himself a frozen pizza and ate it while he scrolled through the information. Two hours later, he stuffed the remains of his dinner in the trash and stretched, annoyed that he hadn't found anything substantial to tie DeLito or Wiley to the thefts. Yet.

His gut instinct assured him he would, though—in time. But his instincts were in a tailspin over Hannah and her sisters and their involvement. His first inclination told him they were innocent, especially Hannah. Why would a respectable doctor involve herself in illegal affairs? Mimi and DeLito seemed pretty tight, although Mimi acted slightly ditzy, so he could see DeLito easily pulling something over her eyes. But if the sisters knew the truth, their close-knit family relationship would explain the motive for their silence. Being the oldest, Hannah had obviously fallen into the caretaker role and would protect her family, including her father, no matter what. Spending time with them on Thanksgiving gave him the perfect chance to watch them all together. He'd planned to go into the dealership early and snoop around, then drop by the house later in the day, but what a streak of luck—Wiley had saved him from inventing an excuse by his invitation.

His mind turned to DeLito. Maybe his connection hadn't been at the dealership during regular hours the past two weeks; maybe they met after the place shut down for the night. Maybe Wiley had no idea what transpired after hours, what DeLito was up to.

The El Camino sat beside his SUV, a beacon of silver in the dim light—and a little too conspicuous for him to drive for surveillance. Hoping for a break in the case, he bypassed the convertible, climbed in his Cherokee and headed toward Wacky Wiley's.

HANNAH DUSTED a cloud of white from her face, sank her fists into the stiff white dough and began to knead, counting the movements for accuracy and wondering what had gone wrong with the first four batches of dough. Her hands ached from pounding and rolling, and her hair had turned a ghostly shade of white. She'd never felt more like a failure in her life, and she hated to fail at anything. She measured some more flour, determined to master this baking thing.

Her cat Oreo sauntered over, sniffed at the crisp black rolls in the trash and wrinkled his nose.

"They're not that bad, are they?" Hannah asked.

Oreo darted under the table as if he suspected she might poison him. "Okay, I admit it, they're pathetic. Horrid. But I can't figure out what I'm doing wrong. I've watched Mimi bake pastries in her coffee shop a dozen times. She makes it look so easy."

A knock sounded at the back and she pushed her hair from her face with a flour-covered arm, then opened the door.

"Hey, sis?" Alison's gaze traveled over Hannah briefly before she burst into laughter. "What have you been doing, having a flour fight with the cat?"

"Making rolls," Hannah said, well aware of the exasperation in her voice.

"But you don't cook," Alison said in an incredulous voice. "At least nothing that doesn't come out of a can."

"I know." Hannah sighed, defeat weakening her voice. "For some crazy reason, Dad told Jake I always made homemade rolls that would melt in your mouth so…"

Mischief sparkled in Alison's green eyes. "So you're trying to impress this guy, huh?"

"No," Hannah said hastily. "It's just…well…" Why exactly *was* she killing herself to make fresh homemade rolls?

Alison gave her a knowing look, popped open a bottle of water and plopped onto one of the bar stools at the counter. With another giggle, she pointed to the trash. "Those look like asteroids."

Hannah rolled her eyes and began to knead the dough again. "Thanks. Between you and Oreo, I'm all confidence here."

"Don't sweat it, Hannah. You can't do everything. I mean, my God, you're a doctor, you graduated with honors from med school, you don't have to cook, too."

"You'd think if I could stitch injured people in the ER, I could at least follow a recipe and bake bread."

Alison's eyes twinkled as she rested her hand on her chin and studied her. "He *is* a hunk, sis. I can see why you're interested."

"I'm not interested." Hannah pinched the dough into balls. "I treated him when he came into the hospital. I simply agreed to follow up on his care for Dad. Dad seems to feel he owes Jake for getting shot."

"Uh-huh. So it's Jake now."

"That's the man's name, Alison."

"Well, whatever it's worth, I approve, Hannah. And I say go for it."

Hannah's gaze swung to Alison's. "I told you I'm not interested in the man."

Alison arched a dark brow. "Sure you're not."

"I'm not! He's not even my type. He's a drifter for heaven's sake. And he sells used cars."

"He certainly is sexy."

"So what? The man roams from one place to another with no plan in his life. I want to establish a family practice here in Sugar Hill, win people's respect."

"He has a great body, too."

"Yeah, but we have nothing in common. I bet he doesn't even like to read."

"You don't count the sport pages?"

"Hardly!"

"He's probably dynamite in bed."

"Well, his kiss is pretty hot, but there's more to life than sex."

"So have you kissed him since that hot one at the car lot?"

Hannah winced. "No. Forget about how sexy he is, Alison. What about love and trust and companionship and hobbies and having things in common to talk about on rainy days?"

"I can't think of anything cozier than cuddling in bed with a sexy man on a rainy day."

"You sound like Mimi. Are you behaving yourself at school, Alison?"

"We're not talking about me," Alison pointed out. "We're talking about you and Jake. I saw the way he was looking at you. He wants you, Hannah. And you had fun with him tonight. Don't be afraid to let go and enjoy yourself."

"I'm not afraid. And it doesn't matter if Jake does want me. I...we aren't right for each other. I can't believe Dad even invited him over." Hannah stared at the odd-shaped clumps of dough, disgusted. "This is hopeless."

"I doubt if Jake cares if you can bake rolls."

Hannah's gaze took in the four batches she'd attempted to make and the dough spread before her, and didn't even bother to reply. Ever since she'd received that hope chest, her life had been turned upside down. With the entire Thanksgiving day looming before her, she doubted the end to the madness was anywhere in sight. She gathered the clumpy dough and tossed it in the trash. Alison's comment about being afraid reverberated through her head, reminding her of Dr. McCoy's comments—nonsense. She wasn't afraid to let go and have fun. Was she?

No. She'd simply go by and pick up some rolls on the way to dinner—she didn't have to impress anyone, especially not Jake Tippins.

Chapter Eleven

Jake drove toward Wiley's the next day rubbing his hand over gritty tired eyes. He hadn't slept much last night. He'd stayed outside the car lot well into the darkest hours of the evening, keeping the place under surveillance in case DeLito showed, but if the salesman had conducted business, he'd met his contacts elsewhere. Of course, DeLito could have gotten wind of Jake's undercover gig and moved the operation to another site. So far, Wiley had seven spin-off used-car lots located in seven different cities. Although police were investigating each of them, they'd all believed the main thrust of the thefts had originated right here in the outskirts of Atlanta—at Wiley's home base.

But the job wasn't the only thing that had kept Jake awake. When they'd been decorating, he'd seen Wiley pull Hannah into his office before she'd left. Through the glass window, he'd watched them speak in hushed voices. Wiley had slipped Hannah a folder which she had tucked under her arm and taken home. What had been in the folder? Records for her to doctor to hide Wiley's illegal deals?

When he'd left the lot, he'd found himself driving by Hannah's house to see if she'd gone home. Worse, he'd contemplated stopping by her place, trusting her with the truth about his job at Wiley's, actually asking her about the files. *Trust* and *truth*—two terms missing from his vocabulary.

Of course, he'd reined in his insanity, knowing he couldn't blow his cover, and sternly reminded himself that he and Hannah were way too different to ever have anything together—except steamy kisses. And great sex.

A relationship—never.

Later, when he'd finally succumbed to fatigue and climbed into bed, sleep had overcome him, scattering all thoughts of the case into oblivion. Fantasies of Hannah had taken over and wreaked havoc with his subconscious. He couldn't allow himself to care about anyone, not with his job, not with his moving around, not with his own family history....

She needed someone respectable, settled, someone who'd know how to socialize with her doctor friends, someone who'd fit in.

All the things he could never be or do.

Damn, the woman was messing up his head. His thoughts had been bouncing back and forth like a boomerang.

Refusing to fool himself into believing any differently, he didn't understand why he still found himself driving by her house on the way to Wiley's Thanksgiving dinner. Hoping to find another man there so he could stop fantasizing about how perfect and innocent she was? Hoping that she might be at home wishing he were there in her bed and arms, loving her and imprinting his own stamp of ownership on her body?

Furious at his wandering thoughts, he slowed the El Camino as he neared her street, scanning the drive for vehicles. Hannah's dependable Volvo sat parked in her drive, the only car in sight. So...Hannah was home.

Working on the files? Or making those damned homemade rolls her father had been bragging about?

He shut out the little voice nagging at him and pulled into traffic, deciding he'd drive slowly so he wouldn't arrive at Wiley's too early. After all, it would be a long day and he needed to plan his strategy. Today he'd have all three Hartwell sisters together—the golden opportunity to glean as much information as he could about their father. Maybe today Hannah would reveal something concrete that would point to her innocence. Or to her guilt.

HANNAH RACED through the Piggly Wiggly, disgusted with herself for being late and roll-less. Regardless of last night's decision to buy rolls, she'd tried again this morning to bake some and failed miserably. When the thirteenth batch had flopped, she'd decided that although she wasn't superstitious and still didn't believe in the lore associated with the pearl ring, she did not have time to try to bake another pan of bread, so she'd dressed for the day, stopped by the bakery and would try to pawn off some of the grocery-store rolls as her own.

Apparently, a lot of other people had the same idea.

There wasn't a single package of rolls left at any of the stores in town. She'd considered calling Mimi, but her sister had her hands full with desserts. The Piggly Wiggly, her last stop, had a loaf of wheat bread and two cans of bake-at-home biscuit dough. She grabbed the cans and headed toward Wiley's, chastising herself for acting so irrationally. She certainly didn't want to pretend to be something she wasn't—Hannah hated phonies—and she *had* baked homemade rolls, they simply had turned out to be black craters or lumpy clumps of inedible dough.

Still, she hated admitting failure, so she was opting for a half truth.

Slowly pulling into her father's drive, she took a deep breath, bracing herself for the sexy used-car salesman/patient/drifter her dad had invited, and heard Alison's words echoing in her head. *Don't be afraid to have fun.*

No, she wasn't. She simply refused to waste time with a man so obviously ill-suited for her. The rock Grammy Rose had put in her hope chest and the note—*don't let the man you marry weigh you down*—confirmed her decision. Wouldn't a man like Jake eventually hurt her?

Extricating herself from the car, she stuffed the paper bag beneath her arm, adjusted the pale blue blouse she'd tucked inside slinky black pants and strolled up the sidewalk. Seconds later, Mimi ushered her inside with a hug. The warm scents of chocolate cake, turkey, dressing and sweet potatoes filled the small house. Alison danced through the doorway, wearing a Braves jersey and juggling a tray of iced tea. The TV blared from the den, the Thanksgiving Day parade filling the screen.

"Grammy Rose!" Hannah exclaimed when she saw her dear grandmother sitting on the sofa. "What a nice surprise. I didn't know you were going to be here."

"Hey, honey, come on in! Alison picked me up." Grammy was sitting next to Jake, her small frame dwarfed by his huge size. Jake's long legs were stretched out on a gray ottoman, his thick black hair spiked haphazardly as if he'd just run his fingers through it.

The room suddenly shrank in size.

Hannah hurried to hug her grandmother. "Don't get up, Grammy." She bent to give her a kiss. "I'm so glad you made it. Are you feeling better? No signs of pneumonia?"

"No, I'm fine, honey." Grammy patted Jake's knee. "This young man has been keeping me entertained."

Jake turned, awkwardly lifting himself to stand.

"You don't have to get up," Hannah said, knowing his injury still made him stiff.

He stood anyway. "Hello, Hannah."

"Hey, sis." Alison sailed into the room with the tray of drinks.

"I have to check on the sweet potato soufflé," Mimi chirped. She winked at Alison and disappeared into the kitchen. Alison handed Jake and Grammy Rose glasses of tea, flipped her hand up and waved. "I have to help Mimi."

"Let me help, too," Hannah said, panicking at the matchmaking twinkle in Grammy Rose's eyes.

"Oh, no, Hannah." Alison pointed a finger at the sofa. "It's way too crowded in there. Sit down and entertain Jake and talk to Grammy. Tell her all about the pearl ring."

"I've already talked to Grammy about the ring." Hannah shot her sister a murderous look and indicated the package in her hands. "And I need to heat these."

Alison snatched the bag. "I'll take care of them." With a mischievous giggle, she flitted away before Hannah could argue.

Grammy Rose chortled at the lively animated characters performing in the Thanksgiving Day parade on the TV screen, as she moved to the rocking chair. "Here, Hannah, you sit by your young man now."

Hannah stifled a gasp. "Grammy, he's not my—"

"Come on, sit down, doc," Jake said, a smile tugging at his lips. "Did you bring those homemade rolls that melt in your mouth?"

Hannah smiled weakly, tapping her fingers up and down her arm. "Actually, they're not. I…I've been at the hospital on an emergency all morning and didn't have time to bake. I had to pick up some store-bought ones. I hope you don't mind."

His jaw seemed to tighten, his eyes darken. "You had to go in this morning?"

Hannah nodded, her pulse racing. She was a terrible liar. Why didn't she just confess the truth about her poor culinary skills?

"I hope it wasn't anything serious," Jake said in a gruff voice.

"No, I mean, there was a small…child…" Hannah struggled for something believable, aware the lies were growing. The very reason she hated them—once you told one lie, you triggered a domino effect and soon things spiraled out of control.

JAKE WATCHED Hannah squirm and tap those fingers up and down in that nervous gesture he'd come to recognize. He knew she'd been home all morning because he'd driven by there twice, then actually waited at the end of the street until he'd seen her pull away from her house—why was she lying? And why did he feel so disappointed when he'd begun to trust her.

"He…uh, was choking on a chicken leg," Hannah said.

"Mercy me," her grandmother exclaimed.

Jake jerked himself back to her lies. "The kid's okay?"

"Oh, yes," Hannah said, averting her gaze away

from his questioning one. "But once I arrived, three other emergencies came in so I stayed. I barely had time to run home and change."

Jake nodded, deciding Hannah Hartwell was one of the worst liars he'd ever met. Put her in an interrogation room and the woman would fall apart.

Put her in his arms and...

Wiley suddenly bounced into the room wearing a bright orange shirt and a hand-painted tie with turkeys on the front. "While we're waiting on dinner, I thought we'd watch some videos."

Hannah groaned. "Not those old videos of us when we were kids, Dad?"

"Oh, let's!" Grammy Rose squealed, winking at Jake. "These girls were such precious little things when they were little. Why, Hannah used to read fairy tales and play dress up—"

"Grammy, I'm sure Jake's not interested—"

"Of course I am," Jake said, grinning at her grandmother. "Your grandmother's a fascinating storyteller. She's already been regaling me with tales about your mischievous toddler escapades. Something about mustard handprints on the walls."

Hannah rolled her eyes, and Jake wondered if she was simply embarrassed or trying to hide family secrets.

Ignoring Hannah's protests, her father popped in a tape. "I still say I should have sent some of these movies to that 'Funniest Home Videos' show."

"But Dad—"

"It's okay, Hannah," Jake said, his mouth twitching. "I don't mind."

Hannah folded her arms across her middle, obviously bracing herself for the mortifying recounting of her childhood. Mimi and Alison bustled in and sat cross-legged on the floor, eager and enthusiastic.

"Where's Joey?" Hannah asked.

Mimi shrugged, looking disappointed. "I don't know. He said he'd be here."

"Shh." Wiley pointed to the TV where a two-year-old Hannah raced across the yard to the kiddy swimming pool, buck naked.

"That was you, Hannah. My, you were a pretty baby," Grammy said. "You never did like to wear clothes."

Hannah sank lower into the sofa, and Jake couldn't fight a chuckle.

"Turn it to the Christmas ones, Dad, or we'll never get to eat," Hannah pleaded.

Wiley fast-forwarded to the Christmas when Hannah was five, Mimi three and Alison a baby. Decorations filled the tiny house, holiday music blared in the background and her father sauntered in dressed as Santa, a huge burlap sack slung over his shoulder. Hannah sat on the floor in the midst of freshly opened packages, toys surrounding her.

"Hannah collects dolls," Alison explained.

"That was a long time ago," Hannah said, her shoulders stiff as she watched.

"You used to line them up and tell them stories," Grammy said. "You told me you'd always want a doll for Christmas, no matter how old you got."

"Well, I grew up, and I don't ask for dolls anymore," Hannah said in a low tone.

"Don't you ever get too old to dream, child," Grammy chided in a loving voice. "Oh, look, there's Cousin Elroy." She clucked her tongue. "You know that was right before he had to go to prison. Best thing that ever happened to the man. He's been honest ever since the state released him. Learned how to bake in the pen. Now he's a fancy chef at one of them swanky places downtown.''

"Is that a fact?" Jake asked. Out of the corner of his eye he saw Hannah shudder.

Grammy slapped a bony hand on her thigh. "Yep. We've had a lot of jailbirds in this family. He wasn't the first of the Hartwells to find himself in trouble with the law. Uncle Roy did a stint back in '89, and Aunt Martha got arrested for burning the flag in the seventies. Of course, she was burning her bra, too. One of them hippies.'' Grammy laughed, obviously thrilled to have Jake's undivided attention. "She's a saleslady at Victoria's Secret now. Sells bras instead of burning them.''

Jake chuckled.

"Grammy, do you have to tell Jake about all the Hartwell black sheep?'' Hannah asked.

Grammy laughed. "Honey, every family's got 'em. Why hide the fact?''

Exactly, Jake wondered, unless she didn't want to raise suspicion.

"Oh, look, Grammy, there's you and Gramps,'' Alison said.

They sat through the next four years, Wiley boasting about each of the girls and how much they'd grown, recounting stories about the gifts they'd begged for and the adventures he'd had trying to locate the more difficult-to-find toys. Hannah finally relaxed enough to laugh as Mimi danced across the screen, wearing her Little Red Hen costume. One year, she'd received a dress-up box with dozens of costumes and they'd put on an impromptu version of Cinderella. Alison had painted the set with her fingerpaint kit while Hannah had added props.

Hannah had been the princess.

Jake's gut tightened at the sweet innocence in her childhood expression; the kind of joy that was missing from her face now.

"You used to love fairy tales, Hannah," her father said wistfully. "You'd climb in that maple tree outside and pretend you were trapped like Rapunzel, waiting on a knight to storm in and rescue you."

"I was only a kid," Hannah said, her cheeks turning pink. "Thank goodness I grew up and stopped living in fantasy land."

"Oh, look, there's the Sleeping Beauty doll you got for your birthday one year." Mimi turned her head, her brow furrowed. "Whatever happened to your doll collection?"

"It's in the attic where it belongs," Hannah said. "Why don't we turn it back to the parade? Jake must be bored out of his mind."

"Not at all," Jake said, enjoying himself. "This is very entertaining."

The next clip featured one of Wiley's famous ads.

"That first ad aired on your birthday, didn't it Hannah?"

Hannah nodded. Jake watched her face cloud over as if she was suddenly lost in memories. Judging from her expression, they weren't all happy.

HANNAH REMEMBERED the day the ad had aired in painful clarity. The Christmas-in-July ad had first been shown on Hannah's ninth birthday—the day her mother had deserted them.

Wiley was dressed like Santa, his big belly shaking

with laughter as he rang bells above all the specials for the month. Her mother had stormed out, her suitcase in hand, just as he'd shouted "Ho, ho, ho" on the screen. Hannah's excitement over the commercial had quickly faded as she'd listened to her mother's tirade. She'd accused Wiley of embarrassing her with his stunts, claiming that if Wiley loved her, he'd end the foolishness and get a respectable job. Maybe even work for her father.

Wiley had balked, saying he'd never be bought by her dad or stuck in a boring office from nine to five pushing papers around a desk, wearing a tie that her father picked out for him. Then Hannah had overheard the reason her mother and her father had married in the first place—the unwanted pregnancy. *Her.*

When Hannah emerged from her memory, she heard Mimi relating the story about their mother leaving that day. Another clip started, taken on the next holiday. The doll collection was suspiciously missing. So was the joy in Hannah's eyes.

A warm hand covered hers, and Hannah realized Jake had slipped her hand under his own. The warm contact sent her nerves skittering in a thousand directions. She stared at their joined hands for several seconds, then lifted her gaze to see him studying her intently.

Thank goodness, her sisters were unaware. They were laughing at Mimi, who had received a toy guitar that day and was dancing across the screen performing *Rudolph the Red-Nosed Reindeer.*

Wiley suddenly jumped up. "I think something's burning."

"Oh, no! It's probably the rolls!" Mimi pushed to her feet and raced toward the kitchen. Hannah saw Alison staring at her hand intertwined with Jake's and quickly jerked it away.

Mimi appeared in the doorway, holding a pan of charred biscuits. Hannah laughed. So much for *her* contribution to dinner—although the ones Mimi held still looked more tasty than her homemade ones.

"DINNER'S SERVED," Wiley announced a few minutes later.

Alison helped Grammy Rose from the rocking chair, and Hannah automatically reached for Jake's arm to help him. He frowned and pulled away. "I can manage."

"Did you bring your doughnut to sit on?"

"I don't need it," Jake muttered through clenched teeth.

"But, Jake—"

A muscle ticked in his jaw. "Drop it, doc. Don't humiliate a man any more than he already has been."

Hannah nodded. "I'm sorry, I simply wanted you to be comfortable."

Jake shrugged. "I didn't mean to snap, but I'm not accustomed to people hovering over me."

"Sorry, I'll try not to hover. But you need to take it easy. Oh, and come in next week and I'll remove the stitches."

His jaw tightened again. "I'll find another doctor if you don't mind."

"Of course not," she said, stiffening. "Now come on, let's eat."

"Lead the way. I'm starved."

Hannah guided him to the maple dining table. Everyone had seated themselves, conveniently leaving two empty places side by side for him and Hannah. Grammy and Alison both giggled. From Hannah's frown, Jake sensed her displeasure over the devilish two who had conspired to play matchmakers. He'd simply have to suffer through the women's devious meddling.

Jake settled himself in the chair a little awkwardly, but the rest of the crew continued chatting about the food and hardly noticed his stiff movements.

"Let's say grace," Wiley said.

The family instantly extended hands. Jake shifted, uncomfortable with the family tradition, but Hannah and her grandmother each took one of his hands to include him.

Wiley began by giving thanks for the food. "And thank you for allowing our family to be together today. We're glad Grammy Rose can be with us. And bless our new friend, Jake Tippins, who risked his neck to protect my business."

Everyone muttered "Amen" while Jake struggled with guilt. He'd never had anyone pray for him and thank him, especially one of his own suspects.

"When did you come to work for Wiley?" Grammy Rose asked.

"A few weeks ago." Jake scooped mashed potatoes onto his plate and tried to make room for Wiley's oyster dressing. "So, how long have you been in the used-car business, Wiley?"

"Let's see, about thirty years now."

"The business has been good to you?" Jake noticed Hannah's wary look, and wondered if his question had hit too close to home.

"We get by," Wiley said with a laugh.

Mimi's gold loop earrings dangled as she turned her head toward the door for the hundredth time. "I wonder where Joey is."

Jake wondered the same thing—was DeLito doing business on Thanksgiving?

"He'll probably show," Hannah said, patting Mimi's hand. "Maybe he overslept or something."

Jake's gaze shot to the bright wall clock shaped like an orange. Apparently Wiley's taste in flamboyant clothes extended to his tastes in furnishings. Was DeLito really sleeping at two o'clock?

"He had to take care of a few things for me this morning," Wiley said, raising Jake's suspicions. "But I imagine he'll be along soon." Wiley gave Mimi an affectionate look. "He wouldn't miss one of your desserts, would he, sweetheart?"

Mimi giggled. "He'd better not, or I'm going to cut him off."

"Mimi!" Hannah's cheeks turned pink.

"From chocolate," Mimi said with a devilish grin.

"How long have you two been going out now?" Grammy asked, her lips pursed.

"Just a couple of months," Mimi said. "I met him at Dad's place."

Alison laughed. "How do you like working at the car lot, Jake?"

Jake's jaw tightened, but he took a sip of tea, trying to disguise the movement. "It's fine. Your dad certainly has a knack for advertising."

"Those early-bird specials are really working," Wiley agreed. "I think we're going to make a killing this year."

Jake thought so too, only he didn't think the profit would be due to the early-bird specials. "Erma Jean's such a sweetheart. Does she take care of all the books?" Jake asked.

Wiley and Hannah exchanged odd looks. Finally, Wiley cleared his throat and replied, "Yeah, I don't know what I'd do without her. You sure do ask a lot of questions, son."

"Sounds to me like the boy wants to get ahead in the business," Grammy winked, as if giving her stamp of approval. "You don't learn things if you don't ask, do you, son?"

"No, ma'am, you don't," Jake said.

"Have you decided to stay here in Sugar Hill?" Alison asked.

Hannah coughed. "Alison—"

"I was just curious." She flipped a strand of her dark hair over her shoulders, her young face full of innocence.

"I don't know how long I'll be here," Jake said truthfully.

"But you're considering staying?"

"I don't know."

"Don't you want to settle down some day?" Grammy Rose asked.

Hannah cleared her throat. "Grammy..."

"I'm afraid I'm not the settle-down type, ma'am. I don't even have a dog, too much to take care of."

"Everyone needs a pet," Mimi said. "I take in strays all the time. Maybe you should think about adopting a dog. They're great company."

"I'm not home enough to take care of an animal," Jake said.

Grammy lifted a forkful of mashed potatoes to her mouth. "So you don't want children of your own some day?"

"I don't know the first thing about kids," Jake said, shifting uncomfortably.

"Neither did I when we had Hannah," Wiley said

with a chuckle. "But a man learns. And these girls have been the light of my life."

"Oh, Daddy," Mimi gushed.

"You're the best," Alison said.

Hannah stared at her plate, her cheeks flushing.

"There aren't any hard and fast rules for parenting," Grammy said. "You learn as you go along."

A knock interrupted the conversation and Mimi sprang from her seat. "It's probably Joey."

Seconds later, Mimi returned with the tall man on her arm. Joey DeLito had thick black hair, combed away from his face, a dark complexion and a jagged scar running along his jawbone. Although DeLito didn't have a record, Jake imagined he was so slick he hadn't yet been caught, or he could be operating under an alias. He turned on his charm with the women customers, flirting with them as if he'd do whatever it took to win their business. He doubted Mimi knew that side of him. He didn't understand why Wiley allowed his daughter to see the man. Jake had taken an immediate disliking to DeLito, and DeLito reciprocated the feeling. Jake would love to bring him down.

DeLito greeted the family, nodding curtly at Jake. "Where have you been, Joey?" Mimi asked, ushering him into a seat. "You missed the home videos."

Joey shrugged. "Sorry. Maybe next time."

"We could show some more after lunch," Mimi suggested.

"No," Hannah replied quickly.

Jake watched quietly as the girls bickered good-naturedly. Grammy Rose frowned at Joey, though, and he wondered if the elderly woman detected DeLito's devious nature.

"Let's have dessert in the den with coffee," Wiley suggested. "I have a surprise for everyone."

The girls emitted a collective groan. "What now, Dad?" Hannah asked.

"I'll show you when we're all settled."

Clearing the table quickly became a group effort, everyone bustling around to carry dishes into the big homey kitchen, bumping into each other and laughing. "Here, let me take your plate, Jake. You go sit down," Hannah said as they turned sideways in the doorway to pass.

"I'm not an invalid," Jake said tightly.

"Look, you're under the mistletoe," Alison squealed. "You have to kiss her, Jake."

Jake looked down into Hannah's face and read panic.

"Go ahead," Grammy Rose said. "It's tradition."

"It's silly—"

"Hannah!" Alison chided. "Kiss the man!"

Jake didn't give her a chance to fight him. He swept his arms around her, lowered his head and claimed her mouth, gently pressing his lips around hers so she had to kiss him back. When they finally pulled apart, Hannah's eyes seemed slightly glazed, stunned. His own breathing sounded erratic.

Alison clapped gleefully.

Hannah darted away from Jake. "Um, let's get dessert."

"Mercy me." Grammy Rose fanned her face with a gnarled hand.

Minutes later, they all sat with coffee and chocolate pecan pie in the den. Grammy Rose perched in the rocking chair, knitting needles and yarn in her hand. Alison stretched out on the floor on her stomach, Joey and Mimi took the sofa, leaving Jake to squeeze onto the love seat by Hannah. He was still thinking about that kiss, remembering the sweet heaven in Hannah's lips, the blazing heat in her body.

But Hannah did not look happy. Her frown grew when Wiley reached for another tape.

"No, Dad, not another one!" Hannah groaned.

Alison waved for her to be quiet.

DeLito slung an arm around Mimi, remaining suspiciously quiet. Wiley punched the remote control button and the screen flashed with images of the group decorating the car lot. Music blared in the background, the camera zoomed across the lot at the lights, recapturing the fun-filled evening. The camera focused on Jake for a moment, and Hannah squirmed. Jake prayed no one else noticed the raw look of hunger between them as they'd conversed.

"I'm thinking of using this as an ad for family specials for the holidays," Wiley explained.

"No, Dad, you can't," Hannah said.

Wiley scratched his head, his eyes narrowing. "Why not, honey? I'm already working on a slogan. Would you sign a waver, Tippins? DeLito?"

Jake opened his mouth to mutter a reply, but Joey protested first. "I'm not sure I want to be featured in an ad."

"Trust me, Dad. It's just not a good idea," Hannah said. "You have to come up with something else."

Jake remained silent, hoping Hannah would save him a reply by convincing her father not to use the clip. He didn't want his face plastered across the southeast on a car ad. It might blow his cover. And if Joey had been using an alias and was masterminding the illegal theft ring, he certainly wouldn't want to be exposed.

But why was Hannah so against the ad?

Wiley walked over and massaged Hannah's shoulder. "Okay, honey, we'll talk about it later. I simply thought a family angle would be nice, and it would tie in with the holidays."

Jake had never been at a family gathering per se, and an odd feeling stirred in the pit of his stomach. Maybe it was the indigestion, he thought, refusing to acknowledge that his sudden bout of emotion might be related to this family and their obvious love for one another.

Like Hannah, he'd stopped believing in fairy tales as a kid. That was something they had in common. It was the very reason he'd reached for her hand—because he'd felt some silent connection.

Only now, he didn't like that connection. He didn't want to *like* Hannah Hartwell or any of her family. Liking them would only make it harder to turn them in. And he *would* turn them in if he had to. Because that was his job, and Jake Tippins lived and breathed for his work.

Hannah Hartwell seemed to be open and trusting and caring and he…well, he plain out wasn't and never would be.

Chapter Twelve

Hannah bristled as she pulled into her driveway, anxious over the fact that Jake had followed her home. Being in close quarters with him all day had been difficult enough—she certainly didn't want him making himself comfortable in her home, imprinting images of his big sexy body in various parts of her house, leaving his husky male scent in the air to torture her.

But when Wiley had shown concern, so atypical of him, Jake had insisted he'd follow her home, just to make sure she made it safely. Jake had done his own share of insisting also—right before they'd left, Wiley had asked her and her sisters to get a tree the next day. Mimi had begged Joey to go, then Jake had insisted on accompanying them. She had no idea why—he'd certainly made his feelings on families clear. He didn't intend to marry or have kids. She wanted both some day.

And why had Jake asked so many questions about her dad's business? She'd sensed tension between him and Joey, too. Maybe Jake was more ambitious than she'd first thought. Maybe he wanted to move up the ladder of success at the car lot and saw Joey as the competition. Could she manage a relationship with Jake if he became a permanent fixture at Wiley's? If he did decide to settle down?

Hannah locked her car and walked up the sidewalk, well aware Jake had parked and was climbing out of the El Camino. Glancing at her neatly manicured lawn, she tried to ignore the fact that, even injured, Jake exuded an air of masculinity that put all the other men in her life to shame. Apparently seeing the shrink hadn't helped her one darn bit. She was still wildly attracted to the man.

"Let me go check out the house," Jake said.

"That's not necessary." She quickly inserted the key, unlocked the door and slipped inside the doorway. "But thanks for making sure I arrived home safely. I don't know what's gotten into my father. I've been on my own forever and he's never worried about me before."

"I told Wiley I'd make sure you were safe and I intend to follow through on my word."

Hannah rolled her eyes. "All right. Check the house and I'll make some coffee."

Jake nodded, quickly checking the downstairs, then hurried upstairs while she worked in the kitchen.

A few minutes later, he appeared in the doorway. "Everything looks okay."

"I told you I'd be fine. My dad's being overprotective."

Jake leaned an elbow on the kitchen counter, his body only inches from hers. "He obviously cares a great deal for you, doc."

Hannah bit down on her lip, knowing she should say something to prove she reciprocated the feelings. She did love her father—only she had trouble showing her affection.

"You were a good sport through all those silly videos," Hannah said instead.

Jake shrugged, his dark eyes hooded. "It looks like you have some pretty good memories of being a kid."

"Better than some children, I'm sure."

Jake shrugged again, a pained look in his eyes. Then she remembered he had no family, and she could have kicked herself. "I'm sorry, I do appreciate my father. It's just he can be overzealous about things."

"Wiley means well," Jake said. "He cares about you and your sisters, you can't fault a father for being concerned about his daughters."

"I guess not." Although he'd claimed he didn't ever want a family, Jake had certainly seemed to enjoy hers today. And he obviously had a handle on how a father should behave—he'd certainly taken care of her tonight. Maybe he really did want a family and was too afraid to admit his feelings. "What happened to your parents, Jake?"

"You don't want to know."

Hannah lifted her hand and brushed a dark lock of hair away from his forehead. "Yes, I do. Tell me."

He jammed his hands in his pockets and stared at her, as if he could frighten her with his story. He'd obviously forgotten she worked in the ER. "My old man skipped out when I was a kid. My mom, well…let's just say she liked men."

Compassion swelled in Hannah's chest. "I'm sorry, Jake. Do you still see her?"

"No, she…she wouldn't have gotten any awards for Mother of the Year. I wound up in foster homes. Learned to pick up and move at the drop of a hat."

"That must have been so hard."

He shrugged as if the past meant nothing, but Hannah

suspected he'd learned his drifter ways from his own childhood. Longing swept through her—she wanted to reach out and touch him, to comfort him. Maybe he secretly wanted that family but was too proud to admit it. "Jake, I—"

He touched his finger to her lips to silence her, his gaze locking with hers. A frisson of awareness rippled through her at Jake's husky voice. "Ancient history. Why didn't you want your dad to use that video for his commercial?"

"The hospital isn't very happy with me right now," Hannah admitted. "The chief of staff warned me to maintain a professional image. I hardly think being in one of Wiley's ads will impress him."

Jake nodded. "Probably wouldn't impress your old boyfriend either."

"Or his parents," Hannah agreed, remembering the sizable contributions the Broadhursts made to the hospital and their displeasure toward her. "They can't have me fired, but they can persuade the chief of staff and some of the other doctors to give me an unfavorable recommendation. And once I finish my surgical rotation, I plan to start focusing on a specialty."

"So you aren't going to stay in emergency medicine?"

"No." Hannah handed him a cup of coffee and poured herself one. "Eventually I'd like to find a family practice here in Sugar Hill."

SHE OBVIOUSLY wanted to settle down here near her family. Perhaps near Broadhurst himself. Jake had no idea why thoughts of Hannah reconciling with the man bothered him, but the realization stung. He envisioned the yuppie doctor waltzing back into her life and giving her everything she ever wanted.

Everything he couldn't give her.

Touching her, loving her, holding her in the night....

Her lips parted slightly, the dawning of desire flickering in the moonlit shadows of the porch, and hunger warmed his body, tightening his chest, shooting all the way to his sex.

Forgetting all the reasons why he shouldn't want this woman, all the reasons he could never have her, he reached out and curved his hand at the nape of her neck. The sweet erotic scent of her longing poured over him as her breath hitched slightly in her throat. Her hair felt like softly spun silk draped across his fingers, her skin the smooth texture of perfection. With his heart pounding in his chest, he lowered his mouth and pressed his lips firmly to hers, inhaling the whisper of her surrender as he claimed her mouth with his.

The kiss should have been soft and gentle, testing the waters, but the hunger in Jake rose so quickly that he felt like a starved man who'd suddenly been tossed a crumb of gourmet food. Her breasts pressed against his chest, her soft curves molded against his hardness in a way Jake had never imagined. She threaded her fingers through his hair and he clutched her body greedily, moaning when she parted her lips and allowed him to taste the coveted recesses of her mouth. His tongue plunged deeper as his hands swept down her back, then lower to cup her bottom. Inhibitions faded to the background as his need grew. His sex swelled, surging against the tight restraint of his pants, his thigh wedging itself between her legs.

Hannah reciprocated by scraping his back with her fingernails, by teasing his lips with her tongue, by planting wild hot kisses along his neck. He felt the urgency in both of them, sensed the chemistry that might explode, knew the ultimate act of loving would be mind-numbing. His hands slid to her blouse buttons, slowly releasing the tiny ovals from their fastenings one by one. Her breath fanned his cheek, hot and raspy as he nibbled at her neck, then dipped his head lower to taste the curve of her breasts. She dug her hands into his hair, and he kissed the fine tips of her breasts through her lacy bra. With a flick of his thumb, he released the front clasp, his heart pounding as her breasts spilled into his hands.

"Oh, Jake."

"You're perfect," he whispered.

Her sweet voice nearly drove him to his knees but he forced himself to love her slowly, to tease the soft rose-buds with his tongue before he drew a taut nipple into his mouth and began to suckle. She arched against him, her legs weakening, so he caught her in his arms. She murmured his name on a sigh of pleasure, and he looked up to see passion heating her face.

The whisper of his name on her lips sent his heart racing again, but his conscience invaded, taunting him with guilt.

Only moments earlier, he'd heard compassion in her voice. Maybe pity. He would not take this woman because she felt sorry for him.

Feeling the heat of his arousal diminish slightly, he gentled his kiss, dropped small butterfly kisses along her cheek, then into her hair. He wanted her so badly he couldn't move.

But he had to walk away.

If she was as innocent as he was starting to believe, he couldn't make love to her without telling her the truth about himself and his reasons for being here. And even if she were innocent, what if Mimi were involved? She and DeLito were pretty close. Mimi didn't have a professional career like Hannah. Maybe the pressure of following along in her older sister's footsteps had gotten to her. If so, Hannah would be crushed.

He gently eased her from his arms and looked into her face. "I'd better go."

She nodded, her eyes widening as if she suddenly realized what had happened and still wanted him; as if she trusted him, making his guilt double. It took every ounce of his self-restraint to leave her standing there alone.

HANNAH'S FINGERS slowly roamed across her lips, the imprint of Jake's hot, sensual kisses still burning through her. Why had she never felt such erotic, wild abandon when she and Seth had kissed? And why had he pulled away?

The question she should be asking herself was—why hadn't *she* pulled away? Why had she let herself get to the point of almost making love to Jake in her kitchen when she hadn't been able to give herself to Seth? She'd guarded her virginity like a treasure all through college and med school, vowing to save herself for her wedding night, yet she barely knew Jake, and she'd let him sweep her into his arms and almost take her on the floor.

Feeling dizzy and slightly disoriented, she stumbled through her den, pausing to pet Oreo. "I am losing my mind, kitty. I have to go back and see that shrink. Maybe he can give me something to alter these weird mood swings." Weird as in hot-in-lust one minute, determined-to-avoid-the-man the next.

She tossed her purse on the counter, poured herself a glass of cold lemonade to cool her body temperature, and lumbered into her bedroom, thinking she should look over that paperwork her father had asked her to check. Moonlight spilled through the sheer curtains, illuminating the hope chest, drawing her into its magical spell. She hovered beside it, momentarily admiring the intricate carvings, the bridal gown, the bride doll her grandmother had given her.

The empty curio cabinet where she'd once stored her dolls loomed silent and lonely in the corner. With a knot of apprehension she slowly lifted the bride doll, spread the lacy white beaded gown down over the doll's porcelain legs, and set it on top of the hope chest. She smiled as the soft lamplight glowed against the bride's creamy porcelain face. White-blond eyelashes, stark blue eyes, lips painted a pale pink. Suddenly wistful from the family trip down memory lane, and still dizzy from the frenzied kisses with Jake, she climbed into the attic and brought down her old collection of dolls.

One by one, she removed the treasured dolls, gently wiping each one with a soft cloth so the porcelain gleamed like new, straightening the delicate clothing as she arranged them inside the curio cabinet, except for the bridal doll which she left sitting on top of the hope chest. Most of the others were storybook dolls, although a few odd rag dolls and soft-sculpted ones had found their way into the assortment. Cinderella, Snow White, Goldilocks, Dorothy from the *Wizard of Oz* with her ruby-red slippers, Little Orphan Annie, Madeline, Pippi Longstocking—all her favorites.

Sweet wonderful childhood memories swept through her, resurrecting silly visions of love and princes and happily-ever-after. The last doll, carefully wrapped in tissue paper, was Sleeping Beauty, the gift she'd received on her ninth birthday. Tears burned the backs of her eyelids as she stroked the long shiny black hair. The old childhood fairy tale flitted through her mind and her fingers went to her lips, a shiver rippling up her spine.

Sleeping Beauty had been awakened by a prince's kiss—just as long-dormant feelings and desires she'd never even known she'd possessed had been awakened in her by Jake's kiss.

JAKE DROVE BACK to the duplex, his mind reeling from unwanted emotions over Hannah Hartwell. He didn't want her sympathy, or her compassion, or her…what exactly did he want?

Her body?

Hell, yes.

But the sultry hot kiss had been so full of yearning, so steeped with a deeper, unbridled yet almost innocent passion, that he found himself wanting more.

Wanting what—her love?

Impossible.

Irritated with himself for letting emotions and guilt even enter his conscience, he hurried inside to call Muldoon and see if there were any new developments in the case. The rose Hannah had given him still sat beside his bed on the battered nightstand, its fragile petals blooming with a fragrant sweetness that reminded him of her soft silky hair and her sweetness—the essence of Hannah.

Knowing he wouldn't be able to sleep, he decided to check out Wiley's. Maybe DeLito had been late because he'd been cooking up another deal. Maybe he would even go back there tonight. The sooner Jake could solve the case and leave Sugar Hill, the better.

He climbed in the SUV and dialed Muldoon while he drove away. His partner answered on the third ring.

"Happy Thanksgiving, bud," Muldoon said in a jovial tone.

"Yeah, yeah, I guess you're celebrating with the rugrats."

"Damn right," Muldoon said. "You know I spend the holidays with my family. I wish you'd joined us."

"I spent the day with the Hartwell family."

"Well, do tell. Anything going on with that daughter of his?"

"Wiley has three daughters."

"You know which one I mean. The doctor you seem so taken with."

Jake grimaced. When had he told Muldoon he was attracted to Hannah? "You're reading between the lines again, partner."

Muldoon laughed. "Yeah, right. Now, tell me about the doc."

"There's nothing to tell. Do you have an update?"

"Always working, Tippins. Maybe you need to get a good woman and settle down."

A little white house with a picket fence and three kids? With Hannah?

"You're the one who told me the chief wants this thing solved before Christmas. I'm working on a deadline here, I don't have time for women."

Muldoon chuckled. "All right. I don't have much, but we did confirm that the dates Hartwell traveled to various cities to tape commercials coincide with dates of major movements of stolen cars."

Jake nodded. "Any of the contacts Hartwell made suspicious?"

"Two of the men he had lunch with in L.A. have

priors for fraud, and his daughter, Mimi, accompanied him on three of the trips.''

Jake heard Muldoon's wife calling him. He wondered how it felt to have a wife at home.

Something he would never know.

''That's it for now. I'll keep you posted,'' Muldoon said. ''Gotta go read my boy a bedtime story.''

Jake thanked him and hung up, his mind envisioning the homey scene, his thoughts straying. He imagined himself reading to a small child, a little boy of his own. Snuggling with a wife after the kids were asleep.

Disgusted with himself, he turned the radio to a country and western song, grimacing as the twangy voice of a popular singer belted out the nineties hit, ''Achy Breaky Heart.'' Just listening to the words reinforced his vow to forget a personal relationship with Hannah.

His heart wouldn't be broken—because he would never *ever* let himself fall in love. Because after love, rejection, pain or heartache followed.

Chapter Thirteen

After Hannah had arranged the collection in the curio cabinet, she dragged herself from her nostalgic state and tried to focus on the paperwork her father had asked her to examine. She'd been studying the figures for over an hour, but something seemed off, just as her father had said. She still hadn't quite figured out the discrepancy when the doorbell rang. Her fingers momentarily tightened over the edges of the folder—who could be at the door?

Jake?

No, he wouldn't be so bold as to come over this late. Not after the way they'd parted.

Uncomfortable, she glanced down at her flannel pj's and frowned. Seconds later, she decided if her guest was Jake, flannel would be best—neither one of them needed the temptation of anything slinkier.

The buzzer cut through the air, ringing two, then three times in rapid succession. Whoever it was seemed awfully impatient. Scrambling into her robe, she hurried toward the door, checked the peephole and saw a tear-streaked face—Mimi.

"What's wrong?" Hannah quickly opened the door and ushered her sister inside.

"I don't know," Mimi wailed, throwing her hands in the air dramatically. "But Joey deserted me again!"

Hannah frowned, handing her sister a tissue to dab at her mascara-stained eyes and puffy cheeks. Mimi looked like a raccoon. "Sit down and tell me what happened."

Mimi slumped into the big armchair and flopped her long legs in front of her, sniffing. "I don't know. We were having a good time, we'd gone back to my place and he loved my dessert."

"I can't believe he could eat anything else after that Thanksgiving feast—"

"Oh, Hannah, honey, you are *so* naive, sometimes I can't believe you were engaged."

Hannah suddenly saw erotic images, only not of Mimi and Joey, but of her and Jake. Irritated, she said, "Sorry, I thought you were being literal. Go on."

Mimi shook her head as if Hannah were a lost cause, jumped up and hurried into the kitchen, then returned with a bottle of wine. She poured them each a glass and made herself comfortable on the sofa again. Hannah ran her finger around the rim of the glass, waiting for Mimi to elaborate.

"Well, like I said, we were enjoying our dessert, then Joey's pager went off and he got up and ran off without even finishing…." Mimi hesitated, actually blushing as if she didn't want to blurt out the particulars. It must have been wicked, Hannah thought, for her sister's cheeks to redden.

"Did he give an explanation?"

"He said he had work to do." Mimi hugged her knees to her chest. "What kind of work is so important he would have to rush off on Thanksgiving to do it? For heaven's sakes, he's not a doctor or even a veterinarian! Used-car salesmen don't have work emergencies.''

Hannah studied Mimi's disappointed expression and wished she had some answers. Unfortunately, Mimi was right. ''So why do you think he left?''

''He's found another woman,'' Mimi said in a shrill voice. ''I just know he's in bed with her right now.''

''Now, Mimi, don't jump to conclusions. You don't know anything for sure.''

''I know the woman's name.''

''Her name?''

''Yes, some floozy named Buffy.'' Mimi downed her drink and poured another.

Hannah wrinkled her nose. She'd discovered a woman's name scrawled in the margins of one of Joey's files that her father had given her, the name *Buffy*.

What exactly was Mimi's boyfriend up to?

JAKE SAW JOEY slip into the used-car lot office. He sank lower into his Cherokee, hoping not to be noticed. Joey had raced up minutes before, jumped from his BMW and hauled inside like a bat out of hell. Jake peered through the glass-encased front of the building, saw lights flicker on and he tracked Joey with his eyes as he darted through the building. Minutes later, DeLito emerged, looking frazzled and out of sorts. He dashed into his Beamer and raced from the parking lot on two wheels.

Jake cranked his Jeep and followed, making sure to keep a safe distance through traffic, always lagging behind a car or two so Joey wouldn't notice the tail. They wound through the central part of town, past a row of warehouses where he suspected DeLito might stop, but the man traveled on, finally pulling in at a local pub.

Jake parked across the street and watched DeLito climb out, his shoulders hunched against the evening wind, his jaw tight. He strode into the bar as if he had a definite purpose. Jake slipped from his Jeep and followed, hiding in the crowd a few stools down so DeLito wouldn't spot him. The stench of cigarettes and sweat surrounded him, country tunes trilling out through an old-fashioned jukebox.

A brassy, hard-edged blonde wearing leather pants and a biker's jacket wove between the patrons and settled in a nearby booth with DeLito. Jake couldn't make out what they were saying, but they ordered drinks and talked in hushed voices. He nursed a beer and tried to figure out the relationship—personal or business? The woman was a distinctive change from Hannah's sister, then again, he'd never seen the connection between Mimi and DeLito. Mimi obviously preferred to live on the edge a little more than her older sister.

DeLito lit a cigarette, blew a puff of smoke in the air and glared at the woman, his other hand pounding the table once to emphasize his words. A few customers nearby glanced their way and DeLito seemed to realize he'd drawn attention, so he leaned toward the woman as if to shield them from curious onlookers. A heated exchange took place, then the woman slid a plain manila envelope across the scarred table. DeLito picked it up, stuffed it inside his leather jacket and hurried away. Jake tossed a few bills on the table to cover his tab and stalked outside, more certain than ever that Wiley's right-hand man was involved in the theft ring.

HANNAH'S EARS still burned from gossip as she drove toward her father's car lot the next day. The nurses' lounge had buzzed with rumors that Seth had left town because he was devastated over their canceled wedding. It was also whispered he'd run off with a nurse from obstetrics. And still others claimed he'd gone to a New Age retreat to lock himself in with a bunch of naked people and rediscover his inner soul. Something about washing and anointing each other's bodies with ginseng oil and singing to the moon....

Of course, the rumors were all false; she couldn't imagine Seth doing anything so outlandish as rubbing any kind of oil over a stranger's naked body, but the chief of staff's look of disapproval when she'd passed him in the hall had scorched her. Maybe she'd have to move across the country to escape the gossip—although she'd probably have to *leave* the country since her dad's ads ran from the east coast all the way to the west, where his latest car lot had opened.

Christmas decorations glittered from the sidewalks, garland was draped around phone poles, and miniature trees lit with white lights were interspersed throughout the town. She steered past the newly erected Christmas-tree lot, past the old-fashioned soda shop and Cindy's Cut & Curl until she reached her father's car lot. She was supposed to meet Mimi and Alison here so they could go tree hunting together. With any luck, her father would go instead of sending Jake and Joey as he'd mentioned the day before.

A laugh bubbled in her throat when she saw the car her father had fashioned as a sleigh. He'd decorated the red Cadillac with bows and garland and candy canes, and he sat on the back wearing a Santa costume, his black-booted feet dangling over into the back seat. Apparently Wiley was offering free Santa visits to the customers' kids, along with candy and a specially designed coloring book featuring a dozen different kinds of cars.

He'd strategically placed a fully enlarged picture of the cover on a huge sign hanging above the makeshift sleigh. Already a line of eager kids snaked through the used cars, while a photographer stayed on hand to capture the tender moment for a mere five dollars. A toddler sat in her father's lap, clutching a half-eaten sucker in one hand, tugging at Wiley's fake white beard with the other. The child was obviously determined to find out if Hannah's father was the real Santa.

A brief moment of insanity passed through her again as her imagination swung into overdrive—she saw a dark-haired little boy with black eyes climbing onto Santa's lap, a little boy who resembled Jake. Her son.

Dear heavens—she was hallucinating.

Shaking herself from the stupor, she parked the car, then saw the real, fully grown man emerging from the building. Jake wore a denim shirt with the sleeves rolled up, revealing dark arms dusted with fine black hair. A pair of khaki slacks hugged his muscular hips and thighs. His shiny black hair gleamed in the sunlight.

The breath whooshed from her chest, and she paused to steady herself before approaching him. The memory of his hot, wild kisses surfaced, sending a tingle of awareness up her spine. For her own peace of mind, she prayed he'd changed his mind and would bow out of the Christmas-tree hunt.

JAKE SAW HANNAH approach and willed himself to behave. He was so close to cracking this case that he couldn't allow himself to become emotionally entangled with the beautiful doctor. Surely he could resist temptation a little longer. Although the sight of her in that pale pink sweater hugging her soft curves and that pair of tight, well-worn jeans sheared his careful control into shreds.

Damn. The morning had been frustrating enough without having his body cramped from unsated arousal. All morning DeLito had been hovering in his office, situated right next to Wiley's, so Jake's plan to explore Wiley's files had been nixed. He'd decided to keep his promise to Wiley and go on the tree hunt, hoping to watch Mimi a little more closely.

But he didn't know the first thing about Christmas trees. He'd never had one before, much less gone and cut one down. Thank goodness he didn't have to play Santa. Wiley insisted they hike into the woods and find a real tree instead of buying one from the tree lot in town. He claimed his daughters believed in tradition. Tradition to Jake meant finding whatever local bar was open and forgetting the cheery day with beer and pretzels.

"LET'S GET that big pine!" Mimi shouted.

"I love it," Alison agreed. "The branches are so full."

"It's too big," Hannah argued.

"No, it's perfect. It'll look great in Dad's den. Don't you think so, Joey?" Mimi asked.

Joey slanted a look at the gigantic pine tree and shrugged. He'd been quiet and moody all day. Hannah wondered if he was two-timing her sister but was too big a coward to tell her.

"Come on, let's cut it down," Mimi said.

"I'll get the saw," Alison offered.

Hannah eyed the height from base to top. "You'll probably have to cut off the top to get the tree in the den." She glanced at Jake, hoping for backup, but he'd staunchly avoided offering an opinion on any of the possibilities so far. And they'd been searching for over an hour. Every tree Hannah found, Mimi refused, saying it was too puny. Mimi always wanted the biggest, gaudiest one she could find. She was so much like their father. Jake's steady gaze didn't waver, as if to say he didn't care one way or the other.

"Please, Hannah, Dad has a ton of ornaments, too," Alison begged. "And I know he bought a new set of lights, I think the package said there are a thousand of them."

Hannah imagined the den filled with the huge tree, the branches shimmering with so many lights they would nearly be blinded. But she couldn't disappoint her sisters, so she finally agreed. "All right, but you two have to haul it in."

Mimi laughed with delight and handed Joey the saw. "We'll cut this one down if you two want to go look for your own tree, Hannah. I've already picked out one for my apartment."

"You want to come with us, Alison?"

Alison gave her a devious look. "No, I think they'll need my help to carry this one. You two have fun."

Hannah bit down on her lip. She doubted it would be a good idea to be alone with Jake in the woods. Of course they were only hiking, hunting for a tree. And it was daylight. And Jake did work for her father, so she supposed he was trustworthy.

"All right," she agreed, thinking they would have a simple, quick trip—completely unromantic.

"Don't get lost," Mimi teased as they started to walk down the path.

Hannah paused. "Maybe we'd better come back another day. It'll be dark soon."

Jake shrugged. "We can come back tomorrow if you want, but I can find my way. All we have to do is look for the North Star."

"Okay, let's go ahead while we're here," Hannah said, knowing every minute with Jake only presented temptation. The fading remnants of daylight filtered through the branches of the trees, creating shadows and slivers of light that danced when the breeze fluttered through the woods. Fresh air steeped with the scents of moss and wildflowers only heightened her awareness of Jake and his masculine musky smell. His stark raw power seemed magnified amidst the quiet serenity and beauty of the woods.

"I'm considering not putting up a tree this year," Hannah said, trying to fill the awkward silence as she traipsed behind Jake. He seemed to have a natural sixth sense for directions and had wound them through the thick of the forest with ease.

"My mother never bothered either. The only tree we ever had was this little silver thing." A chuckle rumbled from his chest. "Looked like a pitiful piece of aluminum foil."

His tone held no accusation or hint of hurt, just quiet acceptance. Hannah stopped, stunned by his words and not sure she liked being compared to his mother. She'd sensed his mother was an awful person, but was she becoming just as jaded?

"Do you want to turn back?" Jake asked.

A shadow fell across his face as he turned to stare at her. Somewhere in the distance she heard a bird chirp, the rustle of leaves as squirrels scampered for food.

Hannah suddenly spotted a tall, sturdy-looking spruce jutting from the ground in the clearing. The tree stood all alone, seemingly abandoned by nature in the twilight. The North Star shone straight above it, reminding her of Jake's comment.

"That one," she said, feeling uncharacteristically emotional. "I think it needs a home."

Chapter Fourteen

Jake parked the Jeep in front of Hannah's, frustrated and tired. He hadn't learned anything about Mimi and Joey from the tree-hunting adventure, except that DeLito was about as enthusiastic a tree-hunter as Jake himself. He also sensed tension between Mimi and DeLito and wondered what had caused the rift.

"Okay, where do you want it?" he asked, juggling the scraggly tree down from his Cherokee. Slinging it over his shoulder, he followed Hannah into her house. He didn't understand why Hannah had chosen the lopsided spruce when the woods had been filled with sturdy pines rich in needles.

"In the den." Hannah led the way through the entrance to the hall. The fine antiques and old-fashioned accessories were so different from his own place he found himself staring at them, studying the details. The family photos on the wall, the lace doilies that looked like they'd been handcrafted by a loving grandmother's fingers.

"Just sit it in the corner by the fireplace."

He lowered the spruce, careful not to knock the antique coffee table and the small tea set spread daintily on the gleaming wood surface.

Within seconds, she'd located a tree stand and he settled the tree inside, frowning when he let go and the tree teetered sideways.

Hannah laughed. "I think it's leaning because the branches are so much fuller on the right side."

He tried to readjust the base, but only managed to make it worse.

Hannah laughed harder. "I'm not sure it's going to stand up straight. I may have to get Dad's old belt."

Jake arched a brow from where he'd stooped. "What?"

"Dad's belt." Hannah dug through the box and produced a strip of green plaid flannel. "Dad used to take turns letting us choose the tree. The first year Alison chose, the tree was so lopsided it would hardly stand. Then Mimi made things worse by hanging all the decorations on one side. Dad had to tie the tree trunk to the wall so it wouldn't fall over."

Jake chuckled, awed by the close-knit family. He stood back, scrutinizing the problem, then dropped down and worked to right it, finally leveling the base off with the saw and aligning the trunk. Hannah rummaged through the box of decorations on the Victorian settee.

"If you need to get going, I can finish," Hannah said.

Did she want him to leave?

"No, I can stay," Jake said, knowing Wiley would still be at the dealership and DeLito and Mimi and Alison were delivering the bigger tree to Wiley's house.

She unwrapped a string of tiny white lights and handed him one end. Odd, how easily they seemed to work together. His height enabled him to reach the taller branches while Hannah draped the lights along the lower ones. Finally, Jake climbed the ladder and placed a white angel on top. Hannah plugged in the lights and the angel and the room lit up with sparkling white lights reminiscent of snowflakes.

"It is beautiful," Hannah admitted.

Hearing the soft admiration in her voice touched a chord inside him. He swallowed, catching the sweetness of her smile as she began lifting ornaments from the box.

"You have a lot of decorations," he commented, surprised that several ornaments seemed to be handmade, not expensive crystal or china or glass balls as he'd expected.

"My dad's a packrat. Every year he gave us an ornament for Christmas," Hannah explained. "He kept all the decorations we made at school, too. And my Grammy Rose sends us a homemade ornament in our stocking each year. She always writes the date on the bottom."

Jake studied the simple reindeer made from a clothespin and felt, the crocheted little pig, the handpainted teddy bears and punched-tin stars. Hannah Hartwell's tree painted a picture of loving family memories—something he'd never had.

He shifted and stared at his hands. Her whole family was starting to get under his skin in an odd way. Not a good sign. Emotions had no place in police work. And neither did getting involved with a suspect or a relative of one.

A twinge of panic hit him. He needed to hurry up and unearth the truth about the car ring before he found himself getting attached to the oddball bunch. *If* it wasn't already too late.

HANNAH HAD TRIED her best to keep the conversation light while they'd decorated the Christmas tree but sharing the nostalgic ornaments had somehow seemed so intimate. Occasionally she'd glimpsed a sadness in Jake's eyes, a longing and hunger both sexual and emotional, a hunger she doubted he knew she could see. He'd revealed a lot about himself when he'd mentioned the aluminum tree, and then again when he'd become melancholy over her description of the handmade ornaments her family traded every year. He wanted his own ornament, his own tree she realized, sadly, maybe even his own family or place to belong. Only she doubted the big proud man would ever admit it.

Maybe she was becoming psychic, she thought, finding the idea not quite as unsettling as she once might have.

Or maybe he was her destiny—her soulmate?

Then again, maybe Dr. McCoy was wrong, and she was wrong about Jake, and she was losing her mind.

If she'd learned anything from her own childhood, she knew that trying to change someone to fit a mold didn't work. Her mother wasn't the settle-down type and they couldn't make her stay—Jake was a drifter and would leave, too.

He flipped off the lamp on the end table, stood back, folded his big arms and admired the tree, his mouth twisting up in a smile. White lights glittered from the tree branches like diamonds. "You did a good job, doc."

"Thanks for your help," Hannah said softly.

His gaze met hers, a reminder of the times their fingers had brushed as they'd hung the treasured ornaments, the way his voice had sounded low and husky as he'd said her name. Desire stirred along her nerve endings, rippling into a tidal wave of need as his dark gaze raked over her.

He was going to kiss her, Hannah realized, when his gaze fell to her lips.

She parted them in anticipation, the heady scent of his hunger like an aphrodisiac to her heart. His hand rose to cup her chin, to trace a featherlight line over her lips, then to slide into her hair. Tilting his head sideways, he threaded his fingers in her hair, drawing her to him with a moan of desire that broke the silence humming between them.

"You are so beautiful," he murmured just before their mouths met. Their tongues collided, mating and dancing in a frenzy; their hands found each other, clinging and holding on as passion erupted, breaking down fragile walls of restraint. Hannah sighed in contentment when his arms embraced her, nestling into his body as if she'd been sculpted to fit against his frame. Her pulse beat wildly as he trailed hot kisses over her neck, as his hands covered her breasts, as his blatant arousal pounded against her belly.

She dug her hands into his hair, sweeping her tongue along his face, groaning in pleasure when his mouth dipped to suck at her breasts through the soft knit of her sweater. "In the bedroom," she whispered, urging him to follow.

He didn't release her, merely walked her backward, his hands and mouth everywhere on her fevered skin. Heat rose in Hannah, nearly setting her ablaze, all coherent thought lost in the moment. His hands slid beneath her sweater to cup her breasts, hers lifted the buttons loose from his shirt. They entered her darkened bedroom, still clutching one another, the air between them humming with sultry looks and touches. Hannah felt something press against her leg, something hard and cold, blocking her path to the bed. She glanced down and, through the dim moonlight streaming in the window, recognized the hope chest.

The dreams of her wedding brought her back to reality.

She'd vowed to save herself for her husband. She'd promised to wait until she'd given her heart before she gave herself. And while she *feared* she might be falling in love with Jake, she'd still only known him a short time.

And she had no idea how he felt about her.

Jake slid his hand to the hem of her sweater and the silly folk legend rose to haunt her. She caught his hands, halting his movements, then slowly looked into his eyes. Shadowed by desire, his eyes had darkened to black, had filled with emotions and turmoil that was almost frightening.

She panicked and pulled away, tears filling her eyes. He toppled backward, bumped his backside against the doorknob.

"I can't...Jake, I'm sorry. Are you all right?" She gestured toward his injury.

He nodded, unaware of the reason she had denied him as he massaged his aching hip.

"I really am sorry," she whispered, hating the quiver in her voice. "But...it's just too soon. I...we barely know each other."

"And we're too different," he said, a low, almost hurt edge to his voice.

"No." Even as Hannah denied his accusation, she knew he spoke the truth, and he could see in her eyes that she knew it. It was the very reason she didn't stop him when he turned and walked away.

ANGER BALLED a knot in Jake's stomach as he drove away from Hannah's—anger that Hannah had been right. He was a fool for allowing himself almost to sleep with her. It would only make things harder for him to walk away. And he *would* walk away. Better to do it with the least amount of damage possible. Why hadn't he been able to control himself?

Maybe passion had momentarily taken its toll, but once daylight had broken she would have regretted her impetuous decision. He was simply a rebound affair for her, someone to ease the confusion over her breakup with Broadhurst. And once Broadhurst returned, she'd be reminded of their differences.

Hell, she'd probably decide she'd been crazy to cancel her wedding and go running back to the man.

He should be glad.

Because somewhere deep inside, he had a feeling if he slept with Hannah, he would lose his heart. And he wasn't ready to give it up—not completely.

Although he suspected his loss of control might be due to the fact that he already had given a small part of it to Hannah.

Details from the case bombarded his musings, confusing him even more. He'd already sent the info about the woman DeLito had met to headquarters. And he still didn't know for sure if Mimi and Wiley were involved. They might already have the proof he needed to wind up the case, and he could leave Sugar Hill this week.

Forcing himself back to work, he hurried home and called his partner.

"Muldoon here.... What the hell are you doing calling me so late?"

Jake grimaced. "I've been out of touch all day. Did

you find anything on DeLito or the woman who met him? I sent her photograph in yesterday.''

''DeLito has an alias, Tony Leery. He has priors for auto theft, fraud, forging signatures, writing bad checks, the list goes on and on.''

Exactly the kind of report Jake had expected. ''What about the woman?''

''All we know so far is that her name is Buffy. I'll call you tomorrow when I find out more.''

Jake hung up, shucked his clothes and went to the refrigerator. Mumbling beneath his breath, he dug through the food Wiley had sent and yanked out contents and made a sandwich. With a beer in one hand and a roast beef sandwich in the other, he slumped onto his sofa and stared at the empty den. Hannah's house had seemed so cozy and full of life, especially with the Christmas tree lighting up the room.

He flipped on the lamp and told himself to get over it. He was alone, always would be. And he didn't mind being alone. At least, he never had before he'd met Hannah Hartwell.

THE NEXT MORNING Hannah saw the Broadhursts walking the halls with the chief of staff, their speculative gazes tracking the ER to make certain things were being run efficiently. A jelly-smeared toddler escaped her mother's hand and barreled toward the soda machine in a nearby waiting area, plowing into Mrs. Broadhurst and wiping jelly on the woman's white pants.

Mrs. Broadhurst shrieked.

Hannah almost laughed. The mother darted forward and retrieved her little escapee, chastising her in a soft voice. Mrs. Broadhurst glared at Hannah as if she'd ordered the little girl to maul her. With rumors still running rampant in the halls, she imagined she'd be getting called into the chief of staff's office any minute now.

She walked past the nurses' station and saw the doors open and a team of paramedics rush in.

"Head injury here!"

"I'm with you," Dr. Porter shouted, motioning the paramedics toward him.

"Patient's going into cardiac arrest!" another team yelled, rushing through the corridor.

Dr. Roberts jogged toward the gurney. "Room five. Get the paddles ready!"

Tiffany hauled around the corner from an exam room, issuing orders to the orderlies and assistants to send for blood and other needed equipment. With a click of her teeth, she glanced at Hannah, her face solemn. "We've got some crazy kook who thinks he's Napoleon in room one. I'm calling psych for a consult."

Hannah sighed. She had just finished a close call with a suicide, had sent the patient to the psych ward herself. Dropping her sterile gloves into the bin, she headed to the locker room, grateful her shift had ended. Pausing momentarily, she whispered a heartfelt prayer for any incoming patients.

She thought of her family as she did so often in the ER. Alison. And Jake.

But Jake wasn't family.

Maybe he could be, a tiny voice whispered. Maybe you should give him a chance—*take* a chance and not be afraid to open your heart.

Guilt plagued her for leading him on the night before, for inviting him to her bedroom, then pushing him away. He probably thought she was some kind of tease. She wanted him to understand her reluctance, that making love to her meant giving her heart. Rationalizing that the hope chest had brought her back to her senses didn't seem to help since the darned hope chest had triggered her migration from sanity in the first place.

She tightened the ribbon around her ponytail, hunched her shoulders and left the locker room, ignoring the curious glances from two nurses. More gossip today—apparently they claimed Hannah had been cavorting around with one of her father's salesmen.

Not too far from the truth. Except they had the information incorrect and had rumored she and Joey DeLito were an item.

She'd have to warn Mimi.

Deciding to get in the giving spirit, she strolled upstairs to the children's ward to offer her services. Seeing the young faces would undoubtedly take her mind off her own problems.

Three children sat in the activity room, cutting yellow stars from construction paper, decorating them with glitter. An elderly volunteer finished reading the last few pages of ''The Christmas Story'' while the children began to work. Hannah listened quietly, stifling a giggle at the globs of glue the little boy dumped on his paper.

''Hey, guys,'' Hannah said. ''Mind if I help?''

The elderly volunteer stood and stretched her legs. Hannah ruffled the little boy's dark hair and smiled at the two girls, then turned toward the volunteer. ''Go take a break. I'll watch them for a while.''

The elderly lady nodded. ''I think I will grab a cup of coffee.''

Hannah collected some of the brightly colored art paper and a pair of scissors. ''I think I'll make one of these, too.''

''I'm making one for my daddy,'' the girl with the

mop of strawberry-blond hair chirped. "He travels a lot."

"And I'm giving mine to my sister. She can't cut, she's just a baby," the little boy said.

Glitter sparkled on the third child's nose, in her hair, all over her fingers as she beamed a toothless smile up at Hannah. "This is magic stardust," the little girl said as she shook another boatload of gold glitter onto her crudely cut star. "And I'm giving mine to my mommy 'cause she's special."

Hannah smiled and began to cut the star shape, already knowing she would give hers away too. To a man who lingered in her dreams, whose quiet masculinity haunted her sanity—a big fearless man who had come out of nowhere and stolen her heart.

JAKE HAD COMBED the town earlier, hunting for abandoned warehouses or property where the stolen cars might possibly be hidden, but he'd come up empty-handed.

Now he studied the files he'd copied from Wiley's computer, relieved he'd finally found a moment to slip into the older man's office, but confused over the segments that seemed to be missing. Suspicions mounting, he guessed they contained information Wiley planned to adjust to cover his underhanded business dealings. He had two more to review when the doorbell rang.

Shocked to find Hannah Hartwell at his door, he simply stared at her, trying to fight the urge to drag her inside and kiss her senseless.

"I have something for you," she said without preamble.

"Not more food," Jake said. "I'm really healed enough, you don't have to—"

"It's not food," Hannah said. She held out a small square of tissue paper and gestured for him to accept the gift. Jake drew his brows together, wondering what the dickens she was up to now.

"It's not much, and you may think it's silly, but I wanted you to have it." A sly little smile lit her face, a soft pink suffusing her cheeks. "As an apology for last night."

"There's no need—"

"Yes," she whispered, cutting him off. "I didn't mean to lead you on. I'm not like that, Jake, not a tease."

"I realize that," Jake said, the vulnerable look in her eyes gnawing at his conscience.

"And it's not that I didn't want you," she said a little too softly, "but I don't give myself lightly."

He licked his lips, striving for a calm voice when his heart was pounding. "I know that, too."

"Then take this. I simply wanted you to know that I was thinking about you, that yesterday was special."

Jake accepted the tissue and opened the folds, stunned to find a handmade glittery star inside.

"It's a Christmas ornament," Hannah said in a rush. "I kept rambling on about all my homemade decorations yesterday, and we made these with the children at the hospital today so I decided… Well, it's pretty crude and you don't have to keep it—"

"It's beautiful," Jake said, his throat suddenly thick. "I'll keep it always." His gaze rose to meet hers, latched onto the emotion in her eyes, and his heart gave a painful tug. First a damn rose. Now a stupid home-made paper star made with glue and glitter. Two silly gifts that melted his normally ironclad control to molten lava.

"You don't have a tree, do you?" Hannah asked.

He shook his head. "I don't usually decorate one."

"Well, maybe you can hang it above the doorway. We let the kids make dozens of them and we hung them from the ceiling of the rec room in the children's ward so it looks like a sky full of stars."

Jake chuckled at her rambling.

She slipped the silky white ribbon from her hair, sending the long golden strands cascading around her shoulders, then brushed her fingers lightly across his palm as she threaded the ribbon through the star. "There, now you can hang it above your doorway."

Jake's finger glided along the silky ribbon, aching to thread his fingers into Hannah's hair. He wanted one more night with her, he realized. A night where he forgot the case and simply savored holding her in his arms.

HANNAH SMILED, biting down on her lip at the less than subtle look of hunger in Jake's eyes.

"Have you eaten, doc?"

Hannah glanced down at her rumpled, worn clothes. "No, but I'm not really dressed to go out. A patient…well, you don't really want to know what happened at the hospital. Let's just say I don't feel presentable enough for a restaurant." She wanted something more private, quiet, so she could mellow out.

"I have an idea. Let's throw together a picnic and go for a drive."

"A picnic?" Somehow that didn't sound like a good idea. *Too* private. Especially with her hormones so out of whack.

"Sure, you do like picnics, don't you?"

"Well, yes, of course, but you—"

"Then come on in, put your feet up and relax for a

few minutes. You can have a glass of wine while I pack dinner.''

Hannah frowned as he took her hand and led her in. ''Listen, Jake, I'm the doctor here. I'm supposed to be taking care of you, not the other way around.''

Jake reached up and gently tucked a strand of hair behind her ear, silencing her protests. ''Then feed my male ego by letting me do this. I'm healing nicely.'' His dark eyes roamed across her face, desire flickering in his lopsided grin. ''You and your dad have been way too generous and I have a lot of energy to expel.''

Hannah narrowed her eyes as he dropped his finger from her mouth and poured her a glass of Chardonnay. Male ego? A lot of energy to expel? Exactly what did the devilish man have in mind?

What did it matter? Hannah decided, catching a glimpse of the pearl ring shimmering on her hand. She'd consider the picnic an act of defiance—by going, she'd prove to herself she wasn't as afraid as Dr. McCoy and Alison had suggested.

Chapter Fifteen

Daylight started to fade as they drove north around the Georgia mountains. Jake's reservations about using Hannah Hartwell thrived full-force. He really thought she was innocent. Or if she was involved at all, she was simply protecting her dad or her sister. Maybe she would even thank him later if DeLito had been using her dad and he exposed the man for his fraudulent behavior.

Yeah, right. She'd thank him for lying to her.

A seed of guilt nagged at him, reminding him he shouldn't become physically involved with the woman until he knew her sister and father were innocent. But temptation in the form of two liquid blue eyes lasered through his resistance. And her words haunted him—*I don't give myself easily.*

But she had almost given herself to him. Did that mean she was starting to care for him?

"Blacktop Bluff," Hannah said, pointing to the magnificent view of the parkway as he pulled into a small park midway up the mountain. A few people lingered in the park, children throwing Frisbees and skipping rocks across the creek. Someone had lit a grill and the steamy scent of charcoal and grilled burgers cooking warmed the chilly air.

"My dad brought us here for a picnic when I was a kid. I remember eating cold fried chicken and biscuits and standing at the overhang in awe," Hannah said. "I thought I could see all of Georgia right here from the top of this cliff, then we drove all the way to the top and I thought I could see the whole world."

"It is beautiful," Jake said, admiring Hannah as much as he did the view. He barely resisted the urge to reach out and stroke her delicate perfect cheek. From the wind blowing in their faces on the drive up, her hair lay in soft whirls around her shoulders. Her cheeks had a rosy glow, her eyes were a little brighter than when they'd first set out. Something had been troubling her, but so far she hadn't opened up. They'd simply listened to a soft blues tape and enjoyed the uplifting ride through the winding countryside in silence. The temperature had been unusually warm for November, but now they'd reached the higher altitude of the mountains, the air had turned nippy. His gaze caught two kids frolicking in the creek, and he had an idea—a little out of character for him, but a way to lighten the mood with Hannah. He wanted to see her smile, to have a few pleasant memories to take with him when he left Sugar Hill. To take some of the seriousness off Hannah's face. To pretend they were a normal couple on a date.

He spread a blanket on the ground, set the picnic basket on top, then gently reached out and tucked an errant strand of hair behind her ear, his voice husky, "I know just what you need, doc."

"What?" Hannah hugged her arms around herself, suddenly suspicious. He had that teasing glint to his smile again. And his lips were so darned close that if she stood on tiptoe she could kiss him. An ache, soul deep, stirred inside her. She started to rise on her toes....

But he caught her hand instead. "Let's go wading in the creek." He gently pulled her down to the grass and began shucking his shoes.

"What? But that water's probably freezing."

"Come on, Hannah, it'll be fun."

Hannah nodded, smiling at the children and picnickers scattered along the edge of the stream. Jake shed his shoes and socks and rolled his jeans up his shins, revealing a layer of dark hair on his muscular calves that sent her imagination into overdrive big time. Hannah swallowed, her nerves fluttering at the sight of his long masculine feet. Everything about Jake Tippins was big—his every feature radiated strength and power and masculinity.

"Well, are you going to remove your shoes, doc, or do you need help?"

Hannah gaped at him. "You wouldn't dare."

The cocky grin he slanted at her indicated he would.

She kicked off her pumps just as he reached for her trouser socks. Shrieking, she pushed away his hands, but he tickled her toes, and she broke into laughter. With a jubilant shout, he yanked off her socks and tossed them aside, then dragged her to a standing position, and pulled her into the icy water. The frigid temperature numbed her other senses as she chased him across the rocks.

"Be careful," Hannah called. "You don't want to fall and reinjure yourself."

"Okay, doc," he called, running faster.

"Jake Tippins, slow down!" Hannah ran to catch up with him, laughing harder when he slipped and almost lost his balance. Cold water sloshed against her ankles and shot icy prickles up her shins. Jake's foot hit a pebble, he yelped and staggered, then lost his footing and fell forward. Hannah shrieked and reached to break his fall, but missed. He caught himself on his hands, landing with his knees splashing in the frigid water, his long body contorted awkwardly as he struggled to maintain his balance and not fall the rest of the way on his face. Laughter bubbled inside Hannah's chest—he looked like a frog as he tried to stand again, his feet slipping, his hands groping on the slick rocks. Finally, when his hand massaged his sore backside, Hannah took pity on him and moved to help him.

Sliding one arm around his waist, she hugged his front with her other and tried to right him. He groaned and grunted and Hannah gasped as his cold hand came up to grab her wrists. They both slipped and almost fell together, but clung to each other, staggering and shrieking as they regained their footing. Lord, the man weighed a ton. Every cell in his body was packed with muscle, too, strong sinewy male muscle that rippled across his chest and back and arms, tightening beneath her fingers. Her body reacted instantly, growing warm at his touch.

Several minutes later, after they'd almost fallen twice, she managed to help him out of the water. They collapsed onto the blanket in a fit of giggles and a tangle of wet arms and legs. "You are a dangerous man, Jake Tippins. I warned you not to wade in the water."

"Playing it safe is boring, doc." He stretched out his legs and rolled to his side so he wouldn't have to lie on his injured backside. Or so she thought. The sharp stab of hunger that flashed into his eyes sent heat bolting through her, replacing the chill of the water with the fire of desire.

Hannah rubbed at goose bumps cascading up her arms, and he grabbed a sweater he'd thrown on the blanket and handed it to her. "Here, put this on."

She gave him an odd look for a moment, as if he'd handed her a rattlesnake, then seemed to relax and accepted the garment. As she slipped it over her head, he couldn't help but notice the way the silky fabric of her blouse molded over lush curves. His sweater swallowed her petite frame, the sleeves dangling over her fine-boned hands. She rolled the cuffs up three times, then flattened the bottom of the sweater over her thighs. He remembered how her bare breasts had looked in the dim light of her den, how soft and sensuous they'd felt in his hands, and he ached to reach out and touch her again.

"This was a great idea, Jake. The fresh air feels wonderful. I'm suddenly starved."

The outdoors reminded him of camping out when he was young, of freedom from his confining house. "Me, too."

Ignoring the innuendo, she opened up the containers of food he'd packed. "Wow, fried chicken, just like old times," Hannah said with a smile. She removed a wine bottle from the basket. Jake grinned and opened the Chardonnay.

Laughter sparkled in her luminous eyes. "I do like wine, Jake, but we have to drive home."

"We'll just have a glass," he promised.

Hannah's eyebrows rose in surprise.

"Don't act so shocked, doc. I may not run in your circles, but I'm not a total slough when it comes to responsibility."

Embarrassment heated her cheeks. "I didn't mean to imply you were. For heaven's sakes, you tackled that guy and got shot trying to be responsible."

"Like I told your dad, I simply reacted. No big deal." He poured them both a plastic cup of wine and took a sip, frowning. "I wish everyone would just let things die down."

Her gaze flashed toward him. "I'm sorry. I didn't mean to offend you."

She was referring to his comment about not running in her circles. Why the hell had he made that stupid comment? "Forget it. Besides," he said, teasing again, "You sounded more like a mother than a doctor."

Her lips tightened momentarily, then she seemed to realize he was teasing and laughter spilled from her lips. Glorious beautiful laughter. "The doctor ingrained in me, I suppose. And I am the oldest of three siblings."

"You are a caretaker, aren't you, doc?"

"I guess so."

Maybe she ought to let someone take care of her, he thought.

But you won't be the one, Tippins.

"Thanks for suggesting this picnic, Jake. I guess I needed an outing and some fresh air more than I realized."

As if deciding she'd revealed something about herself she shouldn't have exposed, she began filling their plates with chicken, potato salad, baked beans and bread. Jake accepted the plate and dug in, suddenly starved.

"You said you had a bad day at the hospital. Working in the ER must be stressful."

She leaned her back against a tall poplar tree and

nibbled at her food. "It is. But the work is rewarding most of the time."

"It has to be hard when you're constantly dealing with life-and-death situations."

Her earlier smile faded. "Yes, but I enjoy helping people."

"It must take a lot of strength to deal with crisis situations the way you do...." He let the sentence trail off, hoping she would pick up the conversation.

"Some days are fine, but others are difficult." She went on to tell him about a teenage boy who'd died in the ER. Sadness crept into her voice, and she picked a blade of grass, playing with the ends while she talked. Jake's heart clenched at the story, visions of all the horrible things he'd seen on the streets bombarding him. He'd thought he and Hannah Hartwell had nothing in common. Maybe he was wrong.

No, he couldn't start thinking like that. Couldn't start liking this woman. Couldn't start imagining the two of them building a life together.

"My heart went out to his parents, you know," she said, as if she should be able to save the world. Her watery gaze lifted to meet his. "There's nothing more important than family."

And he might destroy hers if he didn't clear Wiley and Mimi.

Whoa—when had his job become to clear them instead of to find evidence against them?

"I suppose not," he said, hardening himself to her pain as reality crashed around him.

"I'm sorry, I didn't mean to get so melancholy or be insensitive." She reached out to cover his hand with hers. Her touch was so soft, so gentle and sincere it nearly took his breath away.

Jake shrugged, wanting to steer the conversation back on safe territory. "No big deal."

The anguish in her eyes startled him, because the anguish she felt was for *him*.

"How do you like living in Sugar Hill?"

"It's all right," Jake said, biting into another biscuit with gusto. "Your dad certainly has a booming outfit."

"Yeah, he's excited about the new branches opening up."

Jake shrugged and continued eating, trying to appear nonchalant. "Business must be good for him to expand."

"I suppose." Hannah shifted and tapped her nails along her arms again as if the topic made her uncomfortable. "Although, I don't get involved in the business myself."

Jake frowned; he had seen her take the files home. Why was she lying?

"He certainly gets into those commercials," Jake commented, watching her for a reaction.

"Yeah, he always has." Her eyes flickered shut briefly as if she didn't quite approve of how her father made his money, then she simply shrugged. With a loud sigh, she announced that she was full, emptied her half-eaten plate of food into a plastic bag and stood, brushing at her slacks.

He set his plate aside and studied her as she walked over to the stream. The gurgling brook reminded him of childhood, of a time he'd run away and lived in the woods. Not a happy time, but not one of his more unpleasant memories either.

With her shoulders slumped, her head angled, Hannah looked impossibly small as she leaned against a massive oak. The whisper of her breath in the cool night

air radiated sadness, making him ache for her. Was she
thinking about the patient she'd lost or about her father
and how he made his money? Had he hit on a sore spot
with his questions?

HANNAH STARED into the crystal-clear water rippling
over the jagged rocks and fought off the guilt over her
reaction to Jake's questions about her father. She should
be proud of Wiley. He had worked hard to take care of
the girls after their mother had left. Even though some
of his crazy stunts had brought ridicule to her and her
sisters in their teen years, she knew he loved them. But
a small part of her, that little nine-year-old girl inside
who'd overheard her parents' argument the day her
mother had left, still felt a twinge of resentment at Wiley's choice of careers. If he'd left the dealership, taken
a more subtle approach to business, maybe her mother
would have stayed.

And if her mother hadn't been pregnant with her...

She shouldn't have lied to Jake about helping her
father either. It wasn't like she'd done anything wrong,
only Wiley was embarrassed about his dyslexia, and she
simply checked his numbers before he turned them over
to his bookkeeper to save him from admitting his learning disability. Why, he'd even hidden the secret from
Mimi and Alison as if the learning problem was something to be ashamed of; Hannah had stumbled on the
truth by mistake and had tried to reassure him that his
problem was more common than he realized. But the
big proud man still insisted on secrecy and she'd agreed
to honor his wishes.

Speaking of big proud men...the scent of Jake's co-
logne clung to his sweater, an earthy masculine scent
that filled her with heat and reminded her of the man

who'd brought her here. At least she had one parent and two terrific sisters. Jake Tippins had no one.

"Doc, are you all right?"

Hannah started as she realized Jake had moved up beside her. She'd been so lost in thought she hadn't heard him approach, hadn't even heard a twig snapping. He moved closer, so near she could feel his breath on her neck, could almost feel the heat from his body searing into hers. Then he reached out and rubbed his hands up and down her arms as if to comfort her. Her knees trembled involuntarily, but she tried to ignore the passion simmering between them, aware the other picnickers had left and they were alone.

"Hannah?"

"Yeah, I'm fine." She stepped sideways to avoid touching him and looked up into his dark, serious eyes. "Sorry, I guess the day took more of a toll on me than I realized."

"You don't have to apologize." He reached out and thumbed her hair from her eyes, and Hannah's stomach tightened at the fluttery sensations spiraling through her. His dark eyes roamed greedily over her face. He obviously felt the electricity sizzling between them as strongly as she did. Panicking at the strength of her attraction to him, Hannah tried to pull away. She looked at the trees, then at the clear sky, which had faded into a smoky gray, anywhere she could to avoid Jake's mesmerizing, sanity-stealing eyes.

Jake studied her face, his penetrating gaze unraveling emotions she'd thought long dormant. And awakening hunger unlike anything she'd ever experienced.

His husky voice pulled her into a web of desire as he spoke, "I used to hang out in the woods all the time when I was a kid. Sleep under the stars and make up stories about kids from other planets who lived in another solar system.''

The same way she'd made up stories with her dolls.

The dark soulful look he gave her radiated heat and hunger and hidden secrets. Hannah remembered the crazy silly dream she'd had about this man—that he was her soulmate. Her destiny.

But dreams didn't come true and neither did silly legends. The two of them together—

No, they were far too different…yet were they really? Even in the midst of her busy family, sometimes she felt as if she stood alone.

Her senses begged her to invite him into her heart, but caution warned her to run the other way. He slowly reached out and traced a tender line down her cheek, rubbing his finger in a slow circle across her mouth, and all her reservations died. A groan of protest mixed with surrender rumbled from his chest right before he pulled her into his arms, gently teased her mouth open with his tongue and kissed her.

Chapter Sixteen

With Hannah's soft warm body cradled in his arms, her female scent filling him with desire, Jake completely lost himself in the kiss. Heat flared inside him, searing him with a need so strong he deepened the kiss, tasting the warm vibrant essence of Hannah as she surrendered to his touch. A low moan rose in his throat at the sweet moment, and he dragged her body up against his, plunging one hand into her silky hair while the other stroked her back, the curve of her spine, then traced a path down to her waist. He felt her heart pounding against his chest, his need growing as her breasts flattened against him.

Hand in hand, they slowly moved back to their picnic spot. With a growl of pure male hunger, he lowered her to the blanket, angling himself over her as she looped her arms around his neck. Fire blazed a path down his body as he wedged one knee between her legs, finally breaking the kiss enough to nibble at her chin, then at the sensitive skin beneath her ear. Her breath whispered against his cheek, her hands dropped to grip his shoulders, her sigh of passion overrode all his good sense with an all-consuming urge to take her right there, beneath the stars and the moon and the wide dark sky.

But he suddenly felt her tense—subtle, but oh, so real. Her hands stilled, then swept around to press against his chest. His senses floated back slowly, desire still surging through him, but rational thought finally interceded. He slowed his urgent explorations, not quite releasing her as he pulled himself gently off her. Framing her face with his hands, he dropped a soft kiss on her face, then rolled to his side and simply hugged her against him.

She lay snuggled against him for several long seconds, one hand draped over his chest, while she brought the other one up to touch her mouth. The simple movement, the fact that her fingers were now tracing the tender skin where he'd just kissed her, sent desire burning through him again, a slow, steady ache that threatened to torment him long into the night.

A different kind of desire this time—sweeter, more gentle, but just as strong and potent. And much more disturbing.

"I..." What could he say? That he regretted kissing her.

Hell, he didn't.

Kissing Hannah was the most erotic few moments he'd experienced in years. Maybe ever.

But the fact that she was Wiley's daughter, and he was lying to her slammed into him.

"I—I've never felt this way before," she murmured breathlessly. Her words lingered with a hint of disbelief, as if the kiss had been more than she'd bargained for, maybe more than the ones she'd shared with her fiancé.

Yeah, right.

His imagination was alive and kicking—just like his sexual drive.

He struggled for something to say. The only thing

that came to mind was "I want you," but she didn't look as if she wanted to hear that sentiment at the moment. In fact, she looked confused as if she didn't know how to handle the chemistry between them.

"It was incredible," she whispered.

He was moved by her words, so moved he wanted to give her pleasure, even if he received nothing in return.

He gently traced a finger down her blouse, pulling her to him so their bodies touched from head to toe. He felt her subtle relinquishment of control and his sex hardened, pressing against her. But this moment was for Hannah.

He lowered his mouth and kissed her tenderly with the pure urge to satisfy a woman's needs. His hands caressed her back, stroking and massaging the tender muscles of her shoulders and lower, until he cradled her hips in his hands, pulling her into his male hardness. She sank her fingers into his shoulders, holding him as he lowered his mouth and gently kissed his way down her neck, then slid her shirt up and suckled her breasts through her bra. He unclasped her bra and traced his tongue over a taut nipple, his other hand shifting to slip inside her slacks until he felt her moist heat.

"Oh, Jake, you feel so wonderful," Hannah whispered.

Her passion-laced voice, so full of wonder and joy, sent his whole body into a tailspin of emotions.

"I want you to enjoy," he whispered, moving his mouth to love her other breast, suckling deep and hard as his fingers probed, teased, stroked her femininity.

"Jake?" The soft uncertainty in her voice tore at him.

"Just relax, baby, let it go. Let me love you."

She dragged his head up to kiss him deeply, and he

felt her moan in his throat as her body convulsed around him. Seconds later, she lay spent in his arms, her expression of rapture one he would never forget. But she turned her face to his, a mixture of embarrassment and concern flooding her eyes. Concern that he wasn't satisfied.

"Jake?"

"It's okay," he whispered, against her neck, finally saying the words from his heart. "I just wanted to love you."

Her stunned gaze darted to him. He saw a tiny bite mark at the corner of her ear and silently applauded and cursed himself at the same time. He'd marked her as his, yet he didn't really have the right....

"I'm sorry if I let things get out of hand." He gently reached up and curled a strand of her soft hair around his finger. "But you're pretty irresistible, doc."

"I—I shouldn't have...have let you...." She stood and righted her clothes, moved away to the stream and stared into the gurgling water as if the stony brook held the answers to her confusion.

He studied her rigid back, her slender legs, the slight tilt of her hips outlined beneath his mammoth sweater. If she was using him, she was one hell of an actress. He would almost swear that her innocent act was real. That she was as moved by their lovemaking as he had been. If he told her the truth about his reasons for being here, would she hate him?

But he couldn't tell her, not yet, not until the case was solved.

Struggling to get up on his injured hip, he grunted and groaned until he was standing. Then he slowly walked over to her, his mind whirring with half truths and questions, his body still aching for her.

"Hannah?"

She lowered her head at the sound of her name on his lips. "I—I was engaged only a few days ago."

"But you're not engaged now," he reminded her.

A long silence followed, giving him time to wonder if she regretted calling off her wedding.

"Still, it doesn't seem right." She cradled her arms around herself, shivering. "I—I don't usually go from one man…to another."

She'd started to say from one man's bed to another, but caught herself. He found himself gritting his teeth at the idea of her in bed with that shrink, then silently cursed himself for feeling possessive. He had no right. "Are you planning to go back to him?"

A slight shake of her head indicated no.

"Then you have no reason to feel guilty." He slowly lifted the hair from her neck, massaging the tension from her shoulders. She stiffened at first, then finally sighed and relaxed with the movement.

Finally, she exhaled and faced him. He saw the fine hint of desire still lingering in her eyes, along with a twinge of embarrassment and a truckload of regret. She opened her mouth to speak just as a shrill beep burst into the silence.

Her eyes widened, her hand automatically going to her waist. "My pager." Lifting his sweater, she removed the small object from her belt and checked the number. "It's the hospital, I'm not on call," she said. "But there must be a real emergency."

Was it his imagination or had relief filled her voice?

"I'd better get my cell phone."

He nodded curtly, the call a grim reminder of reality. Even if he wasn't investigating her father, his job didn't exactly invite close relationships. Of course, her job came with odd hours also.

She made the call and turned to him, those blue eyes bright with emotions and questions. Questions he couldn't answer. "I have to go," she said softly. "Over a dozen people have been injured in an apartment fire. They need all the extra medical personnel they can get."

He nodded, quickly packed up the picnic and stored the basket in the back. They rode back to his place in silence, the wind whipping her hair around her face, the cloud of desire and confusion hovering between them. And when she left him at his apartment, he sat in the dark and stared at the blank drab walls, wondering what he was going to do about the sexy doctor.

UNBIDDEN IMAGES flew into Hannah's head as she drove to the hospital—images of Jake Tippins, naked and hot and whispering sweet erotic nothings into her ear. His husky voice murmured all the wicked things he'd like to do to her, and he pledged his love as he held her in his muscular arms. Oddly, he made her feel warm and cherished and safe….

But even if the man was sexy and all alone, even if she did feel sorry for him and even if she did feel she owed him for getting shot protecting her father's business, he was still a drifter. A man who had no obvious roots and claimed not to want any. A man who didn't bother to unpack or get a steady job because he wanted to be able to skip town at the drop of a hat.

A man who had brought her to ecstasy and taken nothing for himself.

But Jake Tippins couldn't be her destiny.

Because, even in the middle of all her muddled

thoughts, she knew one thing with excruciating clarity—roots, responsibility and family meant everything to Hannah.

And the thought of loving someone else and having them walk out was too scary to even imagine.

LATER THAT EVENING, Jake drove toward the dealership, planning to stake out DeLito. Blocking images of Hannah's soft body in his arms took every ounce of strength he possessed. But he saw DeLito leave work, and reminded himself he needed to solve the case before he even considered letting things progress further with Hannah.

Was he actually considering allowing their relationship to progress?

DeLito stopped by his dumpy apartment first, and Jake had almost decided he was wasting his time when the man rushed back out to his car and took off. Jake followed, surprised when DeLito drove toward the northeastern parkway. Thirty minutes later, he wound through the mountains. Jake followed, his gut sensing that he was definitely onto something.

Five miles down the highway, DeLito veered onto a dirt and gravel road through the countryside. Jake lagged behind, waiting till the dust settled behind Joey to follow. He crept slowly along the road, dodging potholes and mud-encrusted rocks, finally stopping behind a cluster of bushes in a wooded area near an old abandoned warehouse. Just the kind of place Jake had been searching for.

Grabbing his camera and binoculars, he eased out of the Jeep, and crept through the woods to get a better view, half expecting, half dreading that he would see Wiley or Mimi appear. Instead, the same brassy blonde

DeLito had met in the bar emerged from the dark shadows of the warehouse, holding a cigarette in one hand, an envelope in the other.

Jake raised his camera and photographed the couple, adrenaline surging through him. The out-of-the-way warehouse would be the perfect spot to hide the stolen cars in transit to the dealerships. They might even have facilities inside to paint the hot vehicles and change the license plates. As soon as DeLito and the woman left, he'd check out the place. Then he'd call in the location and get a search warrant. Tomorrow they'd search the place, maybe even tie up this case.

Now, he simply had to figure out whether or not Wiley was involved—and if his daughters knew about his side business. The memory of Hannah's lips burned through his brain and he doused it with cold reality. The case would be over soon, he'd be history, her former fiancé would probably return, and he'd kiss Hannah Hartwell good-bye forever.

IT WAS ONLY TEN when Hannah returned from the hospital. Weary from work and from anxiety over her attraction to Jake, she let herself in the house, made a cup of tea and changed into a pair of silky pajamas. The bride doll stared back at her from atop the hope chest, clearly reminding her of her broken engagement. And the reason for it. She had to talk to someone.

Would Grammy Rose still be awake? Remembering her grandmother's penchant for late-night movies, she decided to call anyway. If she didn't get some advice, she wouldn't sleep a wink tonight.

Settling on top of her bed, she pressed her fingers to her lips again, the heat of Jake's kiss and her wanton reaction to it lingering with an intensity that startled her.

The phone rang three, four times before her grandmother answered. "Hello."

"Grammy, it's me, Hannah."

"Mercy child, is everything all right? You sound plumb out of sorts."

Perhaps her grandmother was psychic. "I *am* tired," Hannah said, leaning against the bank of pillows covering her headboard. *Tired of living in la-la land.*

She explained about Jake. "I don't understand how I could feel so drawn to him, Grammy. He's not at all the type of man to settle down. He's so wrong for me."

"Are you sure about that, hon? Maybe you only think he's wrong for you. Maybe he's exactly what you need."

Hadn't Dr. McCoy made a similar comment?

Hannah still refused to believe it. "What? A drifter who barely even unpacks when he moves to a new town? A man who sells used cars today and will be doing God knows what tomorrow?"

Her grandmother clucked. "So, this is about his job and your dad, huh?"

"No." Hannah twined a strand of hair around her fingers and sighed. "Not exactly. I just don't see us together. Except well…you know."

"I do know, hon," her grandmother said without preamble.

"Grammy—"

"I may be old but I'm not dead, child." Grammy Rose chuckled. "In fact, a good healthy love life keeps you young. I do believe it's kept my wrinkles to a minimum."

"Grammy!"

"And it's good exercise, keeps the heart pumping."

Her grandmother laughed again and Hannah laughed along with her.

Grammy Rose's voice softened, "If you dreamt about the man while wearing the heirloom ring, then he's your destiny. Might as well quit fighting it." Her grandmother sounded as if she really believed the silly folk legend. "Just follow your heart, hon."

"But what if my heart is confused because of this…this chemistry stuff? What if it's not love, just—"

"—lust?"

"Infatuation. I *am* on the rebound from breaking up with Seth."

"Life is full of surprises, Hannah. Some are good, some not so, but we learn from all of them. Love doesn't come with guarantees, but I do believe that legend has some truth to it. And I saw the way he kissed you—mercy me, child."

That kiss!

"But Grammy, hot kisses don't make a marriage."

"No, but trust and love do."

"But Jake told me he didn't want to settle down, didn't want a family. You heard him at Thanksgiving. He doesn't even want a pet."

"I also saw the hunger in his eyes, not just for you but for the whole family. He enjoyed the Hartwell bunch. A man like that doesn't really want to be alone, hon."

"Then why would he say he did?"

"Some men aren't good with words. Sometimes they say one thing while they really want something else because they're afraid to get involved. Men get their hearts broken just like we do."

Could Jake be afraid?

She remembered the few little things he'd said about

his family, his mother. They'd all let him down. Just as her own mother had, a little voice whispered. Dr. Mc-Coy's words echoed in her head—he'd said she might be afraid because she'd been hurt before, because of her mother's desertion. Maybe she and Jake were more alike than she'd ever imagined.

"Honey, you have to listen to what he says with his heart."

What exactly did Jake feel? She had no clue. Except that he had said he wanted to love her. And he'd un-selfishly given her that love in a physical way, the way men showed their feelings, without asking for anything in return.

Hannah thanked her grandmother, then chatted a few more minutes and hung up. She made a fire in her bedroom, and studied the pearl on her finger, the tiny diamonds glittering in the dim moonlight. Suddenly a knock sounded at the door, and she jumped. She grabbed a robe and hurried to the door, wondering if it might be Mimi again. But, peering through the peephole, she saw Jake standing on her doorstep. Maybe silly dreams did come true, she thought, a tingle of excitement rippling through her. Maybe she simply had to open herself up to the possibilities. A strange feeling washed over her…acceptance maybe.

Fate. Destiny. Whatever. She opened the door and invited him in.

Chapter Seventeen

Jake had no idea why he'd come to Hannah's. He'd talked to his superior, and the search warrant would be issued tomorrow. Although the warehouse had been locked and he couldn't see inside, his instincts told him they would find damning evidence. Afterwards, he'd returned to the drab duplex, seen the handcrafted star Hannah had given him along with that rose that refused to die, and he'd driven straight to her place.

Tomorrow she'd learn the truth about him, know that he'd lied, and she'd probably hate him. But he wanted to spend tonight with her, to pretend that none of the lies would matter. Foolish and irrational, he knew, but he'd been behaving uncharacteristically foolishly ever since he'd met her.

"Jake, don't you want to come in?"

Hannah's soft voice broke him from his stupor, and he nodded, his gaze locked with hers as he followed her to the den. Heat flared in the crystal-blue depths of her eyes, engulfing him in a spiraling staircase of desire. Soft light from a single lamp illuminated the room, highlighting her gold hair with streaks of pale yellow and shimmering on her pink pajamas as if they'd been dusted with gold. A faint hint of roses clung to the air, the sultry scent of Hannah's bodywash. A fire crackled in the background, but he glanced around the room and noticed the den fireplace wasn't lit. "I thought I heard wood burning."

"I made a fire in the bedroom," Hannah said softly. "Why are you here, Jake?"

"I..." Why? Because he'd be leaving soon and he wanted her just once before he left. Wanted to hold her and love her and drive away the emptiness he felt inside before she found out the truth and despised him. Wanted to know how it felt to be surrounded with her love. But he couldn't tell her that or the truth or he might blow the case. Instead he told her part of the truth. "Because I want you. I couldn't get you off my mind."

"I've been thinking about you, too," Hannah said softly.

A slow smile curved her luscious lips, sparking his arousal to life. But his hunger went far deeper than just holding her, possessing her body. He ached to feel her in his arms because she'd already climbed into his heart and embedded herself in the layers of his soul.

The admission, although silent, cost him and panic tore at him. He backed away.

"Don't go, Jake."

The softly spoken request halted him midstride. He stared at her, willing her to change her mind. "You understand what I'm saying?"

Desire riddled with acceptance lit her eyes. "Yes. I want you, too."

"You don't have to do this because of earlier, because—"

"I know." She pulled him toward her, placed a hand

over his heart. "And I'm not. I'm doing it because I want to give myself to you."

The second she voiced the words, he dragged her into his arms. Their mouths met, mated, tongues tangled and danced together, mimicking the intimacy they both desired. He threaded his hands in her hair, a guttural groan escaping him at the way she threw her head back, her smooth skin begging for his kisses. He lowered his mouth and tasted heaven in the sensitive skin of her neck, tasted fire in her burning skin, tasted love in every caress she offered him. Her hands dug into his shoulders, tearing at his shirt, clinging to him as he walked her backwards to the bedroom.

This time there was no stopping. Firelight flickered orange and gold, casting shadows on the lace-draped bed, engulfing the room with the air of intimacy. Her scent sent passion tingling up his spine and he found the tiny buttons at the front of her silk pajamas and began to work them free. She dragged her hands through his hair, planting hot kisses on his forehead, his jaw, his mouth, the fire in her unleashing a demon of desire, out of control. Then he pushed her pajama top away, cupped the soft weight of her breasts in his hand, stroked her nipples to hardened buds with his fingertips. She moaned, clawing at his shirt until he released her enough to discard the garment. Her eyes darkened with hunger as she came toward him, but he held her at arm's length, wanting to look at her.

"Jake..."

He heard the hesitancy in her voice and sweet hunger seared through him, making his muscles and body taut with desire. And restraint. "You're so beautiful, Hannah. I don't think I've ever seen anything so perfect."

She started to speak, but he silenced her with his

mouth, plunging his tongue inside to taste her as he covered her breasts with his hands. She arched into him and he slid his hands to the waistband of her pajamas pushing the fabric down her hips to the floor. She stepped out of them, revealing a pair of pale pink bikini panties, a scrap so feminine and tiny his imagination soared, painting an erotic picture of her naked.

He licked her neck, nibbling down the curve of her shoulder, all the way to her breasts where he gently bit the tips of her ripe nipples before taking one in his mouth. She moaned again, her legs buckling, and he picked her up and carried her to her bed, pausing to look into her eyes.

"You're sure?"

She looped her arms around his neck and kissed his neck, her voice a husky whisper in the darkness, "I've never wanted anyone the way I want you, Jake."

His arousal surged against her hip as he pushed the comforter aside and gently laid her on the bed. With one quick motion, he unbuckled his pants and slid them down his hips, taking his boxers with them. Her eyes widened slightly as she took in his size. A hint of fear, of awe...he wasn't sure which. But passion overrode her anxiety and she reached for him.

His arms and hands found her, his lips tasted every delicious inch of her body until she was writhing beneath him, begging him to fill her. He reached inside the pocket of his jeans, pulled out a foil packet, ripped it open with his teeth and sheathed himself.

She watched the movement, her eyes ablaze with hunger. Then he lifted himself above her, nudged her legs apart with his knee and pressed himself into her.

His heart raced, then stopped when he felt a small resistance. "Hannah?" God, she wasn't a...

"Jake, please, I want you."

Cupping her face with his hands, he held himself in check, studied her face, saw the yearning, the love shining in her eyes, and surrendered to her unbidden request. Lowering his head to whisper sweet nothings in her ear, he tasted the salt of her skin, the heady scent of arousal and his muscles clenched, fighting for control. Wanting to give her pleasure, he lowered his head one more time to suckle at her breasts before plunging into her.

She cried out softly and he stilled, hating that he'd hurt her, but moved by the fact that he was her first. Gently, he lifted his head and looked into her eyes, shaken by the emotions he saw glittering in the expressive depths.

"Please, don't stop," she whispered, frantic now with the onset of her release.

He smiled, male pride warring with tenderness as he began to rock inside her. He teased her unmercifully with his tongue, drove her to madness with his body, tortured her with the soft whisper of his breath in her ear.

Until she exploded. She clawed at his naked back, hugged his aching sex within her, trembling with the force of a sated woman. And her soft cries and moans of rapture sounded so deep and heartfelt that his own passion blazed through him.

HANNAH SNUGGLED into Jake's arms, more content than she'd ever been in her life. Loving Jake had seemed so natural, so oddly tender and potent at the same time, so full of emotions and sensations that she had actually seen fireworks exploding behind her eyes.

Had he felt the same way?

He cradled her against him, his breathing finally steadying, his legs entwined with hers. Sweat dampened the coarse hair on his chest, and the faint scent of sex lingered in the air. One of his hands stroked her back in a tender caress. She noticed a long puckered scar along his upper thigh and wondered how he'd gotten it.

"Are you okay?" he asked.

His husky voice sent another thrill through her. "Yes. That was wonderful, Jake. I...never imagined."

A chuckle rumbled from his chest. She felt her face turning a thousand shades of red. "What's so funny?"

"The virgin tigress. Who would have known?"

"That I was a virgin or a tigress?"

"Either one."

She swatted his chest playfully, and he rolled her to her back and climbed on top of her again, cupping her face in his hands. "Why me, doc?"

The gruff tenderness in his voice sent a rush of emotions to the surface, the first of which she recognized as love. But a drifter man certainly didn't want to hear claims of love, did he? Would he think her foolish and naive if she admitted how she felt?

"You're irresistible," she said instead, earning her a sexy grin. *And I'm finally allowing myself to take a chance on love.*

"Well, that's true." His smile faded to seriousness. "But why not that shrink guy you were engaged to?"

Hannah stared at his chest, uncomfortable.

He tipped her chin up with his thumb. "I'm not trying to make you feel awkward. It's just...I'm surprised, that's all. And touched."

She licked her lips and traced a line across his chest with her finger, aware that he watched the movement and that his sex swelled again against her thigh.

"Hannah?"

"Destiny," she finally said, for lack of a better explanation. "You were meant to be my first." *And if the folk legend comes true, my last.*

SUNLIGHT STREAMED through the window, dappling the room in gold, waking Jake to the reality of the day. And to the reality of what had happened the night before.

He'd made love to Hannah Hartwell with an intensity that had shaken his inner core. A part of him didn't want their union to end.

But today he planned to get the evidence to indict DeLito and to find out the truth about Hannah's father.

A fierce sense of protectiveness surged inside him. She couldn't be involved. He wouldn't allow himself to believe it, not after the way she'd given herself to him the night before. Not after she'd offered him the gift of her innocence.

So why had she lied about the files? About helping Wiley? There had to be some logical reason.

The unanswered question nagged at him. He glanced at her sleeping body, fighting arousal at the sight of her beautiful naked form cuddled beside him, sleeping so trustingly. Would he have to arrest Wiley today? Have to betray the trust she'd put in him by bringing him to her bed?

Aching with confusion, he glanced across the room, found her desk and decided he could slip from bed, catch a peek at the files and have some of his questions answered without Hannah ever knowing he'd suspected her of abetting a crime.

Unable to resist, he leaned over and planted a tender kiss on her cheek, savoring the scent of her sweet body as he climbed from bed and tiptoed to her desk.

HANNAH ROLLED OVER and stretched, feeling content and sated and unbelievably sore. The heady memory of the night before rushed back, sending a delicious rush of pleasure through her. She had made love with Jake Tippins. The man who, according to the legend of her grandmother's heirloom pearl ring, was her destiny. She could think of worse fates, she thought with a smile, remembering all the ways he'd loved her during the night. The real thing had been far better than the dreams she'd had.

She'd promised to save herself for her wedding night, but maybe she'd simply wanted to save herself for the man she loved. And she did love Jake, with or without promises.

Opening one eye, she peeked beside her to see if her lover had awakened, hoping to slip into the bathroom and freshen up before he awoke. But the space beside her was empty.

Cold and empty.

Fighting panic that he'd climbed from her bed and already skipped town, she rolled to her knees and opened both eyes, searching the room. Sunlight lit the hope chest, falling in golden rays across the chaise lounge in the corner, rippled into lines on the wall beside her desk. Her desk—where Jake sat.

He was leaning back in her padded chair, with his back to her, his feet crossed at the ankles on top of her antique stool, his face drawn in concentration. What the heck was he doing? Thinking about what to say? How to handle the awkward morning after?

How to dump her without a scene?

Not wanting to startle him, she slowly slipped from the bed, wincing as her bare feet hit the cool hardwood floor. She was naked also, she realized as chills raced up her body. Why was the room suddenly so cold? Had her furnace gone out overnight?

Slipping into a silk robe, she tied it at the waist, tip-toed over to Jake and slid her arms around his neck, then kissed his cheek. "Good morning."

He stiffened in her arms, his hands reaching up to clutch her hands. "Morning."

His voice sounded clipped.

"What are you doing?" She leaned over him and noticed the files she'd brought home from Wiley spread in his lap. "Jake?"

He released her hands and stood, his broad shoulders drawing back as the mouth she'd kissed and loved so wantonly only hours before now pulled into a fierce frown. "I might ask you the same thing. And this time I want the truth, Hannah. Not more of your lies."

Chapter Eighteen

Anger rippled through Jake. To think he'd thought she was an innocent. Had *hoped* she was innocent. But the files in his hands confirmed the cover-up, so Hannah had to have been helping Wiley. At least protecting him. God, what was he going to do?

He didn't want her to be implicated at all. Didn't want her to have to be questioned, to know he'd ever mistrusted her. Because he cared about her.

Maybe even loved her.

What a mess.

"What lies? What are you talking about?" All evidence of the emotions she'd shared with him the night before vanished. Still, his whisker burns marred her neck and face, reminding him that he'd been in her bed only hours before, touching her, wanting her, needing her.

He still wanted her, dammit. But Jake Tippins wouldn't allow himself to *need* anyone.

"Why are you looking through my stuff?" she whispered.

"I thought you said you didn't help your father?"

Her lips pressed into a thin line. There went those fingers again. Tap, tap, tap along her arms. "I don't."

He arched a brow, his temper rising as he shoved the files toward her. "Don't lie, Hannah. I have the proof right here."

"Proof? Proof of what?" She hugged her arms around her middle, looking lost and small. He steeled himself against her act, knowing good and well he'd fallen for the same performance before.

"Proof that your father is running a car-theft ring. And you're an accessory."

She staggered backwards, her eyes wide. "I don't know what you're talking about."

He waved the file for emphasis. "It's all here. Doctored numbers. Notes on Buffy. Sure, some of the deals are in code, but the evidence is there. What were you doing, trying to protect your father?" He ran a hand through his hair, furious and hurt at the same time.

"You're crazy!" Hannah shouted. "I don't know anything about any stolen cars. And I'd never heard of Buffy until I saw that file."

His gaze swung back to her and he saw fury. But something else—hurt, confusion. And her fingers were perfectly still this time, sinking into her arms.

She ran a shaky hand over her face as if to wipe away his touch. "I do look over my dad's records sometimes, but only because he's dyslexic and too embarrassed to tell his bookkeeper."

Jake narrowed his eyes, studying her. "Wiley's dyslexic?"

"Yes, but no one knows. He reverses his numbers so I check them before he gives them to Erma Jean."

"What about DeLito? Does he know your father's dyslexic?"

"I don't know. He could have figured it out, I suppose."

"And so could the bookkeeper." He slapped his hand on the desk. The bookkeeper could have been helping DeLito all along, not Hannah. "Joey is involved in the car ring," he said matter-of-factly. "He has a prior record, Hannah, an alias. I saw the warehouse where he's been storing the stolen vehicles. And if what you're saying is true, I suspect Erma Jean has been helping him."

"*If* what I'm saying is true?" She sliced her hand through the air angrily. "My father may be a lot of things, Jake Tippins. He may be flamboyant and a little showy in his commercials, but he is not a crook. Besides, if Joey was a thief, how would you know? Did you see him doing something at the dealership?"

"He's involved. I just need to know if your dad or Mimi are in on the deal."

"Mimi a party to a crime? My God, she's as innocent as they come...." Her voice trailed off as if realization was dawning. He saw the moment she put two and two together. She staggered backward, her knees hitting that gold chest at the foot of her bed.

"You're not a car salesman, are you?"

He saw the anger rising in her blue eyes and shook his head.

"And that day you caught that thief, you..." She backed around the chest, almost falling onto the bed. But her eyes darkened when she saw the rumpled covers, his jeans lying on the foot of the bed. A look of pure horror darkened her eyes as if she was sickened by the thought of returning to the place they'd warmed with their bodies only hours earlier. Helpless, he watched her stumble toward the chaise on shaky legs, then sink against the pillow, hugging herself. "You're some kind of cop, aren't you?"

He cleared his throat, striving for calm. "A detective. I've been working undercover trying to stop this theft ring. It's major and it's been spreading, right along with your dad's businesses. That's too big a coincidence to ignore."

Her face paled. "My father asked me to check the books this week. He said he thought something was fishy, that maybe Joey had been messing with the numbers." Her hands clenched the side of the chaise, her knuckles white.

"So Joey and Erma conspired without Wiley knowing?"

"My father is not a crook, he's a wonderful man, a good father, a..." Her voice broke, clogged with tears. "You have to believe me, Jake."

A sharp pain tightened his chest. He did believe her, although trust had never come easily to him. Still, he had to ask, "Why should I believe you, Hannah? You lied to me before."

"About the files?"

He nodded.

"But I explained that."

"What about Thanksgiving morning? You said you were at the hospital all morning, but you weren't. You were at home."

"How do you know?" Her eyes widened again, stark shock setting in. "You spied on me?"

"I—I just drove by."

"*You're* lying now, Jake," she said, her voice growing stronger. "I wondered why someone like you would be interested in me—"

"What do you mean, someone like me?" he asked angrily.

She ignored his anger. "You were watching me, using me to find out about Wiley, weren't you?"

He let the silence be his answer. Guilt warred with the truth, all jumbled together in his head. "I was just doing my job."

"And you use anyone you have to to get the job done, right? Including my family?"

He nodded curtly, hating the anguish settling in her face. "I'm sorry, doc."

Her gaze darted to the bed, her voice low, "You...you could have simply asked. You didn't have to sleep with me to get information."

He had to defend his actions. "Maybe I wouldn't have been suspicious if you hadn't lied."

"My dad is innocent," Hannah said, her chin rising a notch. Still, she bit down on her lip, a gesture he'd learned to recognize, as unshed tears glistened in her eyes. "I lied because I tried all morning to make those stupid homemade rolls and I kept messing them up. I felt like a failure."

He frowned, searching her face. "Why would you lie about something so insignificant as rolls?"

She stood and folded her arms across her chest, her voice a soft whisper. Her voice took on a self-deprecating tone, "Because I can't cook."

"But Wiley said—"

"Wiley likes to exaggerate. We grew up on Mimi's Easy Bake oven recipes."

Jake gritted his teeth. "Why didn't you tell me?"

"Because...I hate to admit failure. I wanted to impress you." Hannah's voice broke. "Which proves that I *am* guilty of one thing—being a fool."

With a sweep of her hand, she indicated the door.

"Now, I want you to get out of here, Jake Tippins. And I don't want you ever to come back."

HE HAD SCREWED UP big time.

Jake drove toward the warehouse to meet his partner, his heart pumping, his mind a mess. He'd tried to locate Wiley first, knowing Hannah might try to warn him about the investigation, but he couldn't find the man. Hopefully, Hannah couldn't either. The devastated look on her face when she'd realized his identity, that he had used her, would be imprinted on his brain forever.

She hated him.

And he didn't blame her.

He'd be a bigger fool than he'd already been if he continued to doubt her innocence. Jesus, she'd been helping Wiley because he was dyslexic. She'd tried to impress him by making homemade rolls, something his own mother hadn't ever bothered to do. She'd given him a damn rose and made him a homemade Christmas star out of art paper and glitter. She'd even signed the freaking thing.

Worse, she had given him a part of herself, her virginity, and if he didn't know better, a little bit of her heart. And what had he done? Thrown it in her face by treating her like a criminal. Deep in his heart, he had known that Hannah took care of everyone else. And now, too late, he realized he wanted to take care of her. Shoulder some of her responsibilities and burdens so she could relax and smile—that heart-stopping, dazzling smile that drove him crazy.

Guilt, deeper and colder than anything he'd ever felt, settled in his stomach like a rock. People like Hannah Hartwell didn't lie.

Hell, he hadn't believed they even existed.

He had to tie this case up today and get the hell out of Sugar Hill. Even if Hannah would forgive him, which he doubted because even good people couldn't forgive such deceit, he wasn't a man who deserved her. She deserved fine things and fancy trips and a man who'd know how to romance her in style. Not some broken-down cop who was as scarred on the inside as he was on the outside.

She deserved someone like her old boyfriend.

Pain cut through him, sharp and relentless, but he pushed it away. The dirt road leading to the warehouse loomed in front of him, gloomy and run-down, flanked by scraggly overgrown weeds and bushes. Snowflakes had begun to fall, a flurry of white that fogged his vision. He steered his SUV down the graveled road, adrenaline starting to churn in his veins as the minutes ticked by, signaling the end of the investigation. And his time in Sugar Hill.

By this time tomorrow, he'd be out of the Hartwell family's life for good.

Chapter Nineteen

The hope chest had started it all, the death of her happy, stable future, Hannah thought miserably as she climbed from the shower and wrapped herself in her big terry cloth robe. She'd furiously scrubbed her body and hair, wanting to wash away the memories, but even the thirty-minute shower hadn't completely cleansed Jake's scent from her skin. The man had deceived her, taken her virginity and stolen her heart. Darn him.

She should never have paid any attention to that stupid legend.

And she should never have let Jake touch her.

She stared at the rumpled sheets, remembering every touch, the way she'd come apart in his arms, his husky whispers, and suddenly she felt ill. Furious, she jerked off the sheets and threw them into a pile in the floor. But would she ever rid herself of the image of him in her bed?

Her gaze fell on the lighted curio cabinet and she laughed, a sarcastic bitter noise that didn't sound as if it came from her own throat. She'd actually started dreaming about all that silly, childish stuff again—comparing herself to Sleeping Beauty. How could she have not seen the signs? No wonder he'd been such a clumsy salesman; tackled that thief like a pro; asked all those questions on Thanksgiving. God, he must have laughed himself silly when she'd given him that sappy home-made Christmas star.

What a naive idiot she'd been.

The tears she'd fought since Jake had walked out spilled over and she finally let them fall.

Angry with herself, she raced to the curio cabinet, yanking out the dolls one by one and placing them in a box. She'd take them to the hospital, let the nurses wrap them up as gifts for the sick children. Maybe they would make some of the little girls as happy as they had her—once upon a time.

Now they only reminded her of her own foolishness.

She paced across the floor, her movements jerky. She should have stuck by her convictions, played it safe, done her job and taken care of her sisters.

Mimi.

Good grief, what would poor Mimi do if Joey wound up in jail? The newspaper would cover it all, another Hartwell happening. She could see the headline—The Legacy of the Hartwell Clan Continues.

A sigh of despair escaped her and she ran to the closet and dragged out some clothes. She didn't have time to nurse her own broken heart. She had to talk to Mimi and warn her father before Jake showed up and threw them all in jail. Of course, he probably expected her to try to warn her father. She had to hurry. Wiley might be an oddball, but he was her oddball dad, and he'd done everything in the world to take care of her. It was her turn to stand up for him.

But what about Mimi? She had been acting so strangely lately, worried about Joey two-timing her and all. What if she fell apart?

Time was of the essence here—she couldn't let either of them find out about Jake's investigation before she had a chance to talk to them. She phoned Alison, hoping she'd sit with Mimi while Hannah went to see her father, but no one answered. She left a hurried message, gripping the phone in a panic. Who else could she call?

Seth. He'd been a good friend for years. He had treated Mimi like a little sister when they were dating. He'd know what to do. He should have returned from the conference last night. And he was the most level-headed person she'd ever known. He'd never done a wild, impulsive thing in his life. Unlike gullible her. She only hoped he didn't despise her too much to help her with Mimi. Quickly punching in his number, she waited, her heart pounding. He answered on the third ring, his voice groggy.

"Seth, it's me, Hannah."

"Hannah?" He cleared his throat. "What is it?"

"I…something's come up. I wondered if you'd meet me at Mimi's."

"What's wrong?"

Hannah explained briefly about the investigation, forgoing any details about her bedroom rendezvous with Jake. "You know how impetuous Mimi is, Seth. You can never tell what she'll do when she finds out he's a crook. And I—I didn't know who else to call."

"She is pretty unpredictable," Seth agreed.

"Then you don't mind? I mean, after what I did to you?" Hannah's voice broke, tears spilling over.

"Shh, Hannah, I don't mind. You know I think of Mimi and Alison as little sisters." He sounded so sincere. "I'll meet you there. And Hannah?"

"Yeah?"

"After we see Mimi, I'd like for us to sit down and talk. Okay?"

"Sure." Hannah's mind raced ahead to her father. "I'll see you in about an hour. I want to go by Dad's car lot first."

"All right. Be careful."

Hannah hung up and hurriedly dressed, grateful her dependable Volvo had power as she drove like a maniac to rescue her father. She couldn't bear to see the man who had raised her and loved her unconditionally hauled away in handcuffs by the man she loved.

No, she quickly amended—by the man she had *thought* she loved.

"THEY HAD a first-rate operation going here, didn't they?" Muldoon said.

Jake grimaced, glad the warehouse held the evidence they needed. "Yep. Everything from paint to phony license plates right under our noses."

"You did a good job, Tippins." His partner slapped him on the back. "In spite of your injury."

Jake glared at his partner's smirk, his stomach still balled in a knot, Hannah's face flashing into his mind.

"I'm sure fingerprints will place DeLito here, and his contact, Buffy Ford."

"That has to be an alias," Jake said, referring to the woman's name.

"One of about twenty. The woman changes names and addresses as often as she does hair color. One reason it's been so hard to nail her. But we have a good lead and I've put out an APB on her."

Jake watched as the team from the crime lab began to sweep the warehouse, dusting for prints, taking samples, doing all the monotonous details that would help them make the case stick in court. "Did you find out anything on Hartwell?"

"Not a thing. The locals say he checks out clean."

Jake nodded, deciding he'd use the direct approach with Wiley. He was tired as hell of lying.

The hair on the back of his neck pricked and an uneasy feeling slid into his gut. Jesus, while he was standing here tying things up, Hannah was most likely on her way to Wiley's. What if Wiley were innocent and DeLito showed up and…

He took off running to his car.

"Where are you going?"

"To Wiley's."

His partner issued an order to the crime lab team, then jogged after him. "I'm right behind you."

"HANNAH, HON, what are you doing here so early?" Wiley poured a cup of coffee, his normal cheerful self.

Hannah's heart squeezed. Why hadn't she appreciated her father more? He'd always been there for her. The day she'd ridden her first bike and crashed and skinned her knee. The day the boys at school told her she couldn't be a doctor and she'd slugged one of them in the mouth. The day her mother had walked out. Even the day she'd canceled her wedding.

He'd loved her and supported her without question. Tears burned her eyes, shame burned her throat. "Dad, I…"

"What is it, baby?" The look of affection brimming in his eyes tore at her.

"I love you, Daddy."

He paused, his hand shaking as he set his coffee cup on the white counter. "I love you, too, hon."

"I know." Hannah suddenly swayed forward and

collapsed into his arms. He embraced her, pulling her into the safety of his hug as if she were a child.

He gently stroked her back, the same way he'd done when she was little. "I do love you, honey. Now tell me what's wrong."

She pulled back and gazed up at him, remembering all the times he'd reached out for her and she'd pushed him away. Why had she been so stubborn?

Because she had been afraid of loving, of being left again. It hurt too much.

He jerked a bright orange handkerchief from his pocket, dabbing at her tears. "Has your old man done something to embarrass you again?"

Hannah nearly choked at the understanding she saw dawning in his eyes. "No, Dad, you...you don't embarrass me."

His right eyebrow lifted slightly as he folded his handkerchief and stuffed it back in his pocket.

Hannah smiled, the bitterness of her mother's parting words fading as she realized the depth of her father's wisdom and love. "I'm sorry. I never meant to make you feel that way."

"And I never meant to make you or your mother ashamed of me," he mumbled in a low voice. "I'm just who I am, honey. That's all I can be."

Hannah pressed her hands to her father's cheeks, looking into his eyes, hoping he could see the sincerity in hers. "I'm not ashamed of you, Dad, not now. Not ever. You're the best father a girl could ever want."

Moisture pooled in his brown eyes, his chin quivering. "Honey, do you know how much I've wanted you to hug me? To hear you say that?"

They both laughed then, soft at first, then a little more relaxed.

"Now tell me what brought this on. You're my tough one, so I know something is seriously wrong. Has some guy hurt you?"

He'd hit closer to home than she'd have guessed. But she wouldn't divulge her humiliating experience with Jake to anyone. Her feelings weren't important right now, only her father's freedom and reputation mattered. "Dad, that man, Jake Tippins, he's not who he says he is."

Her father's eyebrows drew together. "He's not? Then who is he?"

"He's a policeman," Hannah said. "He's been working here undercover, investigating an illegal car theft ring located in the south. He claims that the cars have been sold through your car dealerships."

"I see." Wiley's voice grew soft, resigned, making Hannah shiver.

"He says Joey is involved."

"And he thinks I am, too?"

Hannah nodded, the words too painful to say.

"And what do you think, Hannah?"

"Oh, Dad." Hannah's voice broke. "I told him he was wrong, that you couldn't, that you would never—"

"Well, isn't this a happy little family reunion?"

Hannah jerked sideways, stunned when Joey walked in, his eyes full of fury, his hand holding a gun.

JAKE'S HEART was roaring so loudly he could hear the blood pounding in his ears. Snow flurries still fluttered along the highway, painting the trees and ground with a thin layer of white. So beautiful, exactly like Hannah Hartwell had been in that wedding dress the first time he'd seen her. But she might be in trouble.

He raced into the parking lot and climbed out, scan-

ning the lot to see if Wiley and DeLito were there.
Thank God it was too early for Wacky Wiley's to be
open. He spotted Hannah's Volvo perched in front of
the office and his stomach knotted. Jesus, she'd come
here to warn her father and might have put herself in
danger. Muldoon flew up behind him, easing out of his
sedan.

"You think DeLito's here?"

Jake's eyes raked the lot. "I don't know. He has his
pick of demo cars to drive and never shows up in the
same one twice." He gestured toward the glass-
windowed office.

"I'll cover you," Muldoon said.

Jake nodded and inched inside the building, easing
the door closed so as not to alert anyone of his presence.
Voices drifted from Wiley's office. Wiley's. Hannah's.

DeLito's.

Damn.

He moved forward, channeling his weight so he
barely made a sound on the plush carpet until he hovered near the door. Leaning against the doorjamb, he
peered through the crack. His throat closed. DeLito
stood in the center of the room with a gun trained on
Hannah and Wiley. Fury swept through him, but he held
himself in check, trying to formulate a plan.

"Look, Joey, the locals are on to you," Wiley said
in a low voice. "Hell, I figured out what you were doing
myself and already spoke with the sheriff."

"You're bluffing," DeLito snarled. "You've been
too busy making your dumb commercials to know
what's going on."

"That's not true," Hannah said. "Dad suspected
something was amiss. He asked me to check your paperwork because he didn't trust you."

Terror rippled through Jake. What the hell was Hannah doing, trying to get herself killed?

DeLito's jaw snapped tight as he pressed the gun to Hannah's chin. "I think you'd better shut up, Dr. Hartwell."

Wiley threw a hand up. "Don't hurt her," Wiley said. "She's right, though. I already alerted the sheriff. He's on his way to question you."

"No!" Joey's fingers tightened around the gun handle.

"Look, Joey, leave Hannah out of this. Take me with you," Wiley said, his voice blustering out. "I'll be your hostage until you escape. I have clout in the town, people will listen if I tell them to let us through. You can take one of our cars."

DeLito yanked Hannah in front of him and pressed the gun to her throat. "I'll take both of you." His other hand skimmed down Hannah's side. "I think I've been seeing the wrong sister anyway."

A pained expressed crossed Hannah's face, disgust in her eyes as Joey's hands slid down to pat her bottom. Jake saw red. His life spinning in front of him, being blown to smithereens. He couldn't let DeLito hurt the woman he loved.

Loved?

Did he really love Hannah? Of course he did.

But he didn't have time to contemplate his revelation. He had to act now.

Slipping away from the crack, he decided to use his advantage—the element of surprise. He gestured to Muldoon that DeLito was inside. Muldoon nodded.

Jake pushed open the door and aimed his gun at DeLito. "Drop it, man. The game's over."

The three of them all swung toward him, startled.

Wiley jerked Hannah behind him and Jake rushed Joey. They scuffled on the floor. Within seconds, Jake had confiscated DeLito's gun and had the man pinned to the floor and handcuffed. DeLito's dark-skinned face paled as he snarled back an expletive.

Jake breathed a sigh of relief when he saw Hannah safely huddled in Wiley's arms. "Are you okay?"

She nodded, her eyes huge in her pale face.

Wiley gave him a half-hearted relieved smile. "Thank you, son."

Jake nodded grimly, knowing Wiley wouldn't thank him when he'd heard the whole story. Especially when he realized he'd slept with his daughter.

Chapter Twenty

The next hour flashed by in a buzz of activity. Hannah felt dizzy from watching. The local sheriff arrived along with Jake's partner and his superior to take statements from her and her father. Reporters and the local news team had arrived on the scene, snapping pictures and dragging out camera equipment, trying to interview everyone in sight. Jake had staunchly ordered them in the background, then advised her dad to wait for his attorney before answering the police's questions.

Her father had agreed, although he insisted he had nothing to hide. The local sheriff vouched for Wiley, informing them that Wiley had come to him with suspicions. Jake already had a search warrant for DeLito's home and had discovered a connection between him and an ex-con who'd been swiping the cars in south Georgia and shipping them to the warehouse to be repainted.

Hannah sipped a cup of coffee. She'd seen a different side of Jake, a calm, cool, in-control detective who issued orders he expected others to follow. A man who stood alone and liked it that way, a man who would walk away and never look back. Just like her mother.

In her heart, she knew her dad would be cleared.

But would her heart ever be free of Jake?

All she knew was that it was breaking right now. And with every passing impersonal look from Jake, the tender area cracked a little bit more. Even if Jake really loved her, could she live with a cop when she wanted a safe orderly life? Life with Jake would never be safe....

"If you're through questioning my daughter, I'd like to take her home," Wiley said in a curt voice.

"All right. We may have more questions later, so just make yourself available, Dr. Hartwell," the sheriff said.

Hannah nodded.

Reporters jutted forward, but Wiley pushed them aside. "My daughter is not speaking to the press. I'll issue a statement shortly."

"After we've finished," Jake said, glaring at the story-hungry journalists.

Hannah and her father turned to leave, but Jake stepped in front of Hannah, blocking her way. "Hannah...I—I'm sorry."

Hannah remembered his hands and lips on her body, then the cold reality of learning he had cozied up to her for information. A shudder shook her to the core and her knees went weak again, but she refused to give in to the devastation. She still had to see Mimi.

So she forced her chin up a notch. "I don't want to hear any more of your lies."

Jake flinched as she tossed his own words back at him, but Hannah ignored his reaction as her father cleared the way through the throng of cameras and stalked from the room.

Outside, she saw Jake haul a cursing Joey to the police car. She paused, her dad's hand cupping her arm, as she watched the police car take off in a whir of lights and sirens. Jake climbed in his Jeep, his gaze locking with hers before he closed the door. His expression was unreadable, guarded, cold, as if he'd already distanced himself from her. Maybe he'd never cared at all.

"I'll drive you home," her father murmured.

Hannah shook her head and turned to her father, shutting the painful images from her mind. "No, I'm fine, Dad. But I want to stop and see Mimi. I'd rather her hear about this from me than see it on the news. That is, if she hasn't already seen it."

He nodded. "I'd like to go—"

Hannah pressed her hand along his jaw. "There'll be time for that later, Dad. You have to stay here and gather all your records to show the police. Prove to them you're the good guy your daughters know you to be."

He nodded, his heart in his eyes. Hannah felt tears pressing against her eyelids again and blinked them away. She might have been awed by Jake's heroics when he'd burst into the room and saved their lives, but her father had tried to protect her also, had offered to become the hostage so she would be free. Then again, he'd been taking care of her his whole life, only she'd been too emotionally crippled from her mother's desertion to realize it. It wasn't her fault or her father's that her mother had left—her mother simply hadn't loved them enough to stay. But Wiley had; he'd been the stable one in her life.

He was a real hero. And from now on, she intended to show him her gratitude and love.

JAKE DROVE TOWARD the police station, an ache soul-deep pressing in his belly and spreading through his whole body. Hannah hated him.

He didn't blame her, but his heart was splitting wide

open—because he loved her. He hadn't realized how much until he'd seen Joey DeLito's hands all over her, until the slime had shoved that gun to her throat.

He followed along behind the police car, trying to forget the hurt he'd seen in her eyes. The betrayal. For the first time in his life, he'd let someone sneak under his skin, into his heart, and he couldn't pry her out. Now he knew the reason he'd never let himself become involved with anyone before.

Because it was too damn painful. And his job, the very reason that had brought them together in the first place, the only thing he'd ever been committed to in his life, had just torn them apart. And so had his lies.

HANNAH KNOCKED on Mimi's door, her hands trembling. To her surprise, Seth greeted her and walked her to the living room where Mimi sat on the sofa wearing a hot pink silk robe, her knees hugged to her chest, nursing a drink, something that looked like orange juice. The TV droned softly in the background, a weather report about an impending ice storm. But in her heart, the storm had already hit. And she had ice running in her veins.

Seth crossed the room and sat down beside Mimi, gently patting her knee. Hannah was stunned to see Mimi clasp Seth's hand and give it a squeeze. Seth really was a wonderful guy.

She had to thank him.

Before she had the chance, Seth approached her. "Are you all right?"

"Yes, Seth. Thanks for being here."

"No problem. You know your family means a lot to me." He reached out and gave her a hug. "And so does your friendship, Hannah."

Hannah's eyes filled with tears. "You're so great, Seth. I'm so sorry if I hurt you."

"Shh." He pulled her into his arms and hugged her. "You just take care of yourself, okay?"

When he pulled away, Hannah nodded. He kissed her cheek, said good-night and let himself out. Hannah went to talk to her sisters.

Alison sat cross-legged on the floor in jeans and an FSU sweatshirt, her expression a mixture of bewilderment and shock. "I got your message and came on over."

Mimi looked up at Hannah through watery eyes. "Have a mimosa with me, sis?"

Hannah ran a hand through her tangled hair and smiled, accepting the drink from her sister. "Sure, it's been a hell of a day so far."

"You and Dad were awesome," Alison exclaimed. "What a scene, the two of you and all those cops and reporters."

Hannah grimaced, grateful they hadn't seen Joey with the gun pressed to her throat.

"It was all over the news. Are you all right?"

Hannah smiled, touched by the concern in their eyes. "Yeah. I'm sorry about Joey, Mimi."

Mimi shrugged, then held out her arms and Hannah gave her a hug. "He's a jerk. I was about to dump him anyway."

Hannah laughed, realizing she'd never loved her sisters more. "It looks as if our dad can't stay out of the limelight."

"He's so cool," Alison said. "I can't believe he'd already figured out what Joey was up to. And I know Dad didn't like him but I thought it was because he suspected Joey of two-timing you."

"Dad told you Joey was two-timing me?" Mimi asked.

"No, I told him I suspected he was. Dad said he'd keep an eye on him." A smile tipped her lips. "Dad is pretty protective of us, you know."

Mimi laughed and she and Hannah mumbled agreement. "I had no idea Joey was into that stuff," Mimi said. "The little sneak. Using Dad's place to fence stolen merchandise. I must have been blinded by lust not to have noticed."

"I know the feeling," Hannah said.

She hadn't realized she'd spoken aloud until both her sisters' mouths dropped open.

"You slept with the cop, didn't you?" Mimi asked.

Hannah winced and sipped her drink. "Afraid so."

Alison draped a comforting arm around her shoulders. "Well, if it's any consolation, I thought he was a hottie myself."

"Was he good in bed?" Mimi asked.

Hannah rolled her eyes. "Mimi!"

"He must not have been," Alison said. "What a disappointment."

"No, he was great in bed," Hannah mumbled. Her face flamed when she realized what she'd admitted.

Mimi and Alison laughed. "I never suspected he was a cop, Hannah," Alison said. "Did you know?"

Hannah picked at a thread on her sweater. "No, of course not."

"What kind of gun does he carry?" Mimi asked.

Hannah shook her head. "A big-caliber one, Mimi."

Mimi's eyes crinkled as she burst into laughter.

Hannah realized the double entendre and laughed herself, grateful to dispel the tension.

"So, you weren't in on the sting from the beginning?" Alison asked.

Hannah rolled her eyes. Leave it to her sisters to romanticize the entire disaster. Maybe they had a little of Wiley's character embedded in their personalities. She actually considered lying so no one would know what a fool she'd been, then again, she was talking to her sisters. And one lie would lead to another.

She stood and poured herself another mimosa, grateful she wasn't on call. And hoping she still had a job. "He was only using me to find out about Dad."

"I can't believe it," Mimi said.

Alison stood and paced the length of the room. "And I thought he was the perfect guy for you!"

"Did he say he was just using you?" Mimi asked, her voice rising with anger.

Hannah shook her head. "Not exactly. But it's true. He dated me to investigate Dad. I caught him looking at some of Dad's files this morning after…" She closed her eyes, realizing she'd given herself away.

"He slept with you last night and arrested Joey this morning!" Alison pounded her hand in her fist. "The slimeball."

"We'll kill him," Mimi said. "Just name the day and time, sis."

Hannah laughed again, the pain in her chest easing a little at her sisters' support. "He's not worth it."

"Don't let him get you down, Hannah," Alison said.

"Yeah, you're better than him," Mimi said.

Hannah wagged a finger at Mimi. "And you're better than Joey."

"Men are scum," Mimi muttered.

"Dogs," Alison added. "Dirty, slimy, mangy dogs."

"Right and we deserve someone better, someone really hot like Brad Pitt or Matt Damon or…"

"Or Christian Slater," Alison added.

Mimi's eyes lit up. "Or Ben Affleck."

"Or Mel Gibson," Hannah added with a giggle. Only Jake's face flashed into her mind, and, as handsome as the actors were, they didn't melt her heart or make her body yearn the way the lying detective had.

THE NEXT DAY Jake decided he had to see Hannah. He drove toward the hospital, thinking about the past twenty-four hours. The case had tied up nicely. Wiley had been cleared of suspicion, the bookkeeper had been questioned and had admitted to fudging some numbers for DeLito for a hefty payment, and DeLito had confessed. He also claimed Mimi was totally unaware of his actions. DeLito had sung the names of his contacts in the other cities, hoping to cut a deal for a lighter sentence.

Jake felt as if he'd been sentenced himself—as if he'd lost something vital to him, some part of himself that could never be replaced.

He still couldn't shake the memory of the hurt in Hannah's eyes. He realized now that he'd reacted so angrily to finding the files in her house because he'd been afraid. Their lovemaking had been so intense and emotional he'd panicked when he'd felt himself falling in love and contemplating becoming a part of a couple—something he knew nothing about.

But he could learn. After all, Muldoon had a family. What had Grammy Rose said about parenting? *You learn as you go along.* Maybe he and Hannah could learn about this relationship thing as they went along.

He parked his Jeep and walked up the steps to the

hospital, barely limping, but desperate to see her before he headed back to the city. She knew about families, not him. Maybe they could talk. Maybe she could help him find a way to make this relationship work. If she could forgive him....

The ER seemed unusually quiet when he entered. He scanned the hallway and nurses' station but didn't see Hannah anywhere. Two nurses hovered over the paperwork, a tall gangly doctor conferred with a patient in a wheelchair, then he spotted the big nurse who'd first helped him when he'd been shot. He made his way over to her.

"Well, hello, there, Mr. Tippins. How's the hip doing?"

"Fine, Tiffany." He leaned against the nurses' desk. "I need to have the stitches removed. Is Dr. Hartwell in?"

She arched a brow. "I think so. You sure you want to see her?"

He nodded, grimacing at the wary look the nurse shot him. Apparently she knew about his undercover work—did she know he'd slept with Hannah?

Surely not.

"I'll see if I can find her." She ambled off down the hall, her wide hips shaking as she walked. Paramedics rushed through the door and the ER came alive as the tall doctor and a group of nurses rushed toward the incoming patient. This time, instead of seeing the differences between him and Hannah, he saw the similarities. They'd both chosen professions to help people, only Hannah's had far more of a personal touch. They both were dedicated to their jobs, both dealt with life-and-death situations, both had to drop their personal lives sometimes to meet duty. Wouldn't that factor help them understand one another? Support each other? He'd heard Muldoon talk about those kinds of things before. Maybe he and Hannah could make a marriage work.

Whoa—*marriage?*

"Jake, what do you want?"

He hadn't heard Hannah approach. But he heard the anger still hard in her voice. Shaken by the thought of marriage, he faced her. "I need to have my stitches removed."

She folded her arms across her slender waist. "I thought you were going to find another doctor."

"I changed my mind. I want you."

Her lips pressed into a tight line. "Then follow me."

He cleared his throat and did as she said, glancing around the small exam room, remembering the first time they'd met. He'd thought she looked like an angel.

Now, she was looking at him as if she would murder him.

"Lie down on the table."

He nodded. "I—I'd like to talk to you if you have time."

"Lower your pants, please."

Judging from the icy tone of her voice, not exactly an invitation, he thought ruefully.

She slipped on plastic gloves and searched the medical tray for an instrument while he humbled himself on the paper-draped exam table. When he was settled, she walked toward him, no hint of emotion or personal feelings evident.

"This shouldn't take long. You may feel a slight sting but it shouldn't hurt." With that said, she pressed a gloved hand on his hip and began to yank out the stitches, none too gently.

He gritted his teeth, knowing he deserved her anger. "Hannah—"

"It's Dr. Hartwell."

"Hannah," he said between clenched teeth, "I want you to know how sorry I am if I hurt you."

The tweezers pressed into his skin as she yanked another stitch. "I'm assuming you're leaving town."

This wasn't going as well as he'd hoped. "I'm heading back to Atlanta, yes." He tried to prop on his hand and angle himself to look at her. "But I don't want to leave with things so rocky between us."

"Rocky?"

"Tense," he said. "I really want to see you again."

"That won't be necessary." She pulled out the last stitch, wiped his healed wound with a gauze pad and stepped away. "Your injury is healed. I can't think of any reason you'd return to Sugar Hill."

"To see you."

She gave him a scathing look. He rolled farther to his side and reached for her hand, but she crossed her arms and simply stared at him. "Hannah, please. Can we go someplace and talk? Have some coffee maybe?"

"We have nothing to talk about." Her eyes narrowed. "That is, unless you have to ask me more questions about my dad—"

"No, I want to talk about us."

"There is no us." Her beautiful blue eyes stared at him, emotionless. "So go back to Atlanta, Mr. Tippins, where you belong." She gave him one last cutting look. "You know I can't believe I ever felt sorry for you for being alone. Now I understand why you are."

Jake's heart cracked as she turned and walked out the door. She closed it behind her as if she'd closed the door permanently on any hope for a future between them.

Chapter Twenty-One

A week later, Jake roamed the streets of Atlanta, trying to put the Hartwell family out of his mind. Especially Hannah.

The case was solved, all the stolen cars accounted for, DeLito and his accomplice Buffy were both in jail awaiting trial. Things were back to normal.

Quiet, dull, lonely normal.

Only Jake had never been lonely before. Alone yes. But never lonely.

Not the deep sort of lonely that had kept him awake at night, had made him think about the Hartwell Thanksgiving, all the silly traditions they had at Christmas, the freshly cut tree trimmed in homemade ornaments, the woman who'd tried to make him homemade rolls then lied to impress him.

A hundred stars twinkled above him in the inky sky, reminding him of the Christmas star Hannah had given him. He found the North Star, then searched the sky for other constellations, desperately trying to erase her from his mind. Snow clouds were nowhere in sight, although record cold temperatures ranged throughout the south. The coldest December Atlanta had ever seen, the coldest Jake had ever felt in his life.

Christmas decorations glittered from the shops, music drifted from speakers, inviting people in to warm their hands and browse. Cars and holiday shoppers ripped past, everyone in a holiday frenzy.

But Jake had nowhere to go. And no one waiting for him when he arrived home.

He'd wanted the anonymity of the crowd, the isolation, yet now that he had it, even in the midst of the busy street, the emptiness echoed around him. Hannah hadn't wanted him.

She'd walked out of the hospital room that day and no matter how many times he'd called over the next few days she hadn't answered. She'd left him as easily as his mother had.

No, he reminded himself. Hannah was nothing like his mother. Her hesitancy to make love for one thing. She'd even told him she didn't give herself freely, yet she'd given herself to him. Because she loved him— that would be the only reason for a woman like Hannah to finally let herself be taken by a man.

Hope flickered briefly, sparking his determination to win her back again. An antique shop drew his eye, reminding him of the furnishings in Hannah's house. Old lace doilies, period pieces of rich oak and mahogany, a tapestry rug that might have fitted in her foyer. Next door, he spied another shop. A toy shop—no, a specialty shop, a shop full of dolls.

He vividly recalled the collection in Hannah's bedroom—he'd briefly paused to study them that morning when he'd risen, before he'd read those blasted files.

Maybe his guilt would leave him if he had some closure, if he bought her a gift of apology, a little something to prove that he hadn't just used her, that his feelings for her were real.

Hunching his shoulders against the wind, he dug his hands into the pockets of his leather bomber jacket and threaded his way through the crowd until he could slide through the doorway. The smell of apple cider and cinnamon warmed the air, the sounds of children's laughter and Christmas music drifting through the crowded shop. Rows and rows of frilly dolls filled the store—soft sculptured dolls, antiques, replicas of movie stars, characters from movies, baby dolls, Cabbage Patch Kids dolls, dolls unlike any he'd ever seen. A beautiful bride doll stood enclosed in a case, similar to the one Hannah had perched on that gold chest at the foot of her bed. Then his gaze found the storybook dolls Hannah collected. He wandered past, grinning at a little girl hugging a Raggedy Ann to her chest, and stopped at the shelves, mentally ticking away the ones Hannah already owned. Cinderella, Sleeping Beauty, Goldilocks, Dorothy.

The Tin Man and the Cowardly Lion stood beside Dorothy and he suddenly grinned, thinking how he'd loved the characters as a child. If he had the courage to risk rejection, the heart to tell her how he really felt, could he and Hannah make a marriage work? Even though he knew nothing at all about families, could they be a family, the way she and her wacky father and her sisters were?

Without thinking twice, he made his selections and headed to the front. He'd box them up and send them to Hannah with a note, an apology that would let her know he hadn't forgotten her. He glanced up at the Christmas tree in the corner and saw the gleaming star radiating its light—and he thought of the star Hannah had given him, of the North Star he'd been taught to use to guide him home.

He suddenly, desperately, wanted a home with Hannah.

HANNAH CRAWLED into bed, exhausted and alone. Memories of Jake lingered in her house, in her heart, in her mind, keeping her awake long into the night. When she finally slept, she dreamt Jake was lying beside her, whispering sweet nothings in her ear, telling her to take a chance, not to be afraid.

She jerked awake and sat up, staring into the darkness, shivering with the cool temperature in the house. She hugged her arms around her chest, wishing she could get warm, but she'd been chilled to the bone ever since Jake had walked away. Disgusted with herself, she slipped from bed, dragged on her thick terry cloth robe and stared at the bride doll sitting perched on the hope chest—the beautiful heirloom piece which her grandmother had meant to bring happiness.

But the legend associated with the pearl ring had brought her nothing but heartache.

She pulled the ring from her finger, stared at the tiny diamonds, the intricate setting, frowning at her earlier thoughts. Had the ring and the legend really brought her heartache or had it been her own fault? Her own insecurity? She had been afraid to take a chance, to branch out and try a relationship with someone who didn't fit the picture-perfect mold. But look what had happened when she'd taken the chance. When she had followed her heart. She'd been hurt, used, abandoned.

She quickly placed the ring back inside the small velvet box and packed it into the hope chest with the blue garter. She wrapped the bride doll carefully back inside, then enclosed her grandmother's bridal gown within the velvet-lined walls. She hoped that Jake's memory would be locked away as well.

JAKE WAS GOING CRAZY. His old apartment seemed even more bare and lonely than his place in Sugar Hill had. He couldn't stop thinking of Hannah for more than five seconds at a time. He'd even gotten himself a dog.

A roly-poly overactive little puppy from his partner's chocolate labrador's latest litter. He'd named him Toby after Toby Tyler, a little boy he'd seen in an old movie on cable when he'd stayed up watching the late show because he couldn't sleep.

The fat pup nipped at his feet and Jake picked him up, laughing when the dog licked his face. What would Hannah think about the furball? What would a little boy, maybe his own son, think of the pet? Would Hannah take it as a sign he was ready to settle down?

No way to find out but to call. For the third time that day, he picked up the phone and punched in her number.

HANNAH LAY stretched across her bed, exhausted, fighting a headache. The ER had been crazy all day and she hadn't slept the night before for thinking about Jake. She'd been hard on him that last day when he'd come to have his stitches removed. And she'd refused his calls all week. Was she wrong not to give him a chance? Should they try and talk things through?

The phone rang. Her head was pounding so hard she couldn't bear to answer it and talk to anyone, especially her overconcerned family. But, knowing it might be the ER, she rolled sideways and reached for the handset. The answering machine clicked on, and she paused when she heard Jake's voice.

"Hannah, it's me again." A pause. "I've been trying to reach you for days and…I guess you're still upset." Another pause. His breath filled the line, a little unsteady. "I just wanted you to know I still want to talk, that I'm sorry. And…oh, I got a dog. A little chocolate lab pup. His name is Toby."

He paused again. "Well, give me a call if you want to talk."

Hannah squeezed her eyes shut to stem the tears as the phone clicked into silence. Why had Jake called? Just to say he was sorry; to tell her he'd gotten a dog?

Chapter Twenty-Two

"What are you doing here?"

Jake grimaced. He hadn't expected Wiley to greet him with open arms, but he...well, hell. He didn't know what he'd expected. Had Hannah told him about their relationship?

Jake stuffed his hands in his pockets, eyeing Wiley's Santa suit. "I...we need to talk."

Wiley tugged on his beard, scratching at the puffy white cottony mass. "I thought your business here was finished."

"Look, Wiley, I know you're probably mad I didn't come clean with you up front, but—"

"You thought I might be the head of the theft ring, didn't you?"

"At first," Jake admitted.

"At least you're not lying about that."

"I'm done with lies." Jake poured himself a cup of coffee simply to have something to do.

"I can forgive you for thinking I might be guilty," Wiley said, glaring at Jake. "But you suspected my daughters might be involved."

"I had to check out everyone," Jake said. "That was my job, Wiley."

Wiley studied him, his frown at odds with the jovial costume he wore. "You hurt my daughter, son. Hannah didn't deserve that."

"I know." Jake's chest tightened, his legs feeling a little wobbly. "That's why I'm here. I'd like to make things right."

"How do you think you can do that?"

"I…" The red outfit complete with shiny black boots and a big bag for gifts suddenly gave him an idea. "I want to talk to Hannah. Apologize. Grovel."

"Groveling might work." The corner of Wiley's fake white mustache twitched. "What makes you believe she'll listen?"

Jake folded his arms across his chest. "Because I think she loves me."

Wiley's fake white eyebrows wagged. "And how do you feel about her?"

"That's what I'd like to talk to Hannah about, sir." Jake took a deep breath, then explained his plan.

HANNAH WALKED through the corridors of the ER to the hospital lobby, well aware gossip trailed her every step. Her canceled wedding had only lit the fuse, beginning an explosion of fiery rumors that had escalated with the shakedown that had occurred at her father's car lot.

So much for the tame, subdued lifestyle she'd planned.

Life holds no guarantees, Grammy Rose had said. Laughing at the irony, she tossed her head, trying to seem oblivious to the stares from the nurses on the floor. In a few minutes, the Christmas party for the kids would start and she wanted to be there. She spotted the Broadhursts exiting the elevator and took a deep breath. Seth followed.

The minute he saw her, he waved her over, but the chief of staff caught him in the hall, postponing the dreaded meeting. She'd known Seth had wanted to talk since that night with Mimi, but she hadn't been able to face him yet.

What if he wanted a reconciliation? In her heart, she knew she didn't love him. She cared for him, admired him both as a friend and as a doctor, but Seth deserved a woman's total love and commitment. Something she couldn't offer.

Because her heart belonged to another man.

Damn Jake Tippins.

Her reprieve ended when Seth strode toward her. She watched the Broadhursts follow Dr. Porter to the atrium and wondered what they were scheming.

"Hannah, we need to talk." Seth gently clutched her arm and guided her to the open area where she noticed a large portion of the hospital staff had gathered, probably to help with the Christmas party. Dr. Porter stood at the forefront, the Broadhursts frowning as they settled on a love seat adjacent to the small microphone.

Microphone? What in the world...?

"Seth, what's going on?" Had he somehow arranged her dismissal?

No, Seth wouldn't....

Seth leaned close to her as if to guard their conversation. "Hannah, I care about you, you know that, don't you?"

Her stomach twisted. "Yes, and I care about you, but—"

He held up his hand to stop her. "Let me finish. I

admit I was shocked and a little hurt when you called off our wedding.''

Hannah reached for his arm and squeezed his hand. ''Seth, I'm so sorry. I never meant to hurt you.''

Quiet understanding filled his eyes. ''I know. And I still think of you as a dear friend. In fact, I realize now you were right. We are friends and always will be, but we shouldn't have gotten married. I'm glad you were smart enough to figure that out before we both made a big mistake.''

''Then you don't hate me?''

''I could never hate you. I really do care about you, Hannah,'' Seth said in a sincere tone. ''And I want you to be happy.''

Hannah's eyes teared up but she blinked back the emotions. ''You're a great guy, Seth. Someday you're going to find a woman who deserves you. I hope I'm around to congratulate her.''

He drew her into his arms and hugged her. ''Thanks, Hannah. I feel the same way about you.'' He gestured toward the crowd. ''And now, I plan to put a stop to all these stupid rumors.''

Hannah pointed to the podium. ''You called everyone together?''

''You're damned right. I'm sick of everyone saying I've been meditating with a bunch of nude snake charmers. I'm going to set the record straight right now, and I'm going to make sure my nosy parents stay out of our lives from now on.''

Hannah reached up and kissed him on the cheek, smiling as he strode toward the mike.

JAKE STOOD in the shadows of the corridor, hiding behind a cart full of flowers and potted plants, his confidence rocking as he watched Hannah and Seth cuddle together in the hall. He hadn't been gone a whole week yet, and Broadhurst had already tried to crawl back into Hannah's good graces.

But *he* was the man she'd climbed into bed with and he didn't intend to let her bounce back and fall into another man's arms. At least not without knowing exactly how she felt.

Sneaking a peak at the Santa costume he'd confiscated from Wiley, he grimaced, wondering if his idea had been a little on the lame side. He wasn't sure he could play Santa, had never even been around kids much, but he'd thought if Hannah saw him in a Santa suit she might see the good side of him and even forgive him. He wanted her to teach him about family and raising kids.

And he'd come bearing gifts. Both for the kids' Christmas party, which was the reason Wiley had been dressed as Santa in the first place, and for Hannah, the dolls he'd bought and brought with him.

Another lame tactic, but hell, he was only a man and he'd stoop to anything to win another chance with Hannah. Hefting the heavy burlap sack over his shoulder, he adjusted the padding in his belly, hiked up his red velvet Santa pants and headed to the children's rec room for the party.

HANNAH HELPED settle the twenty-plus children into the children's rec room, adjusting IVs and wheelchairs for the in-house patients, gathering the less severely ill kids on the floor in front of the others. Several nurses and doctors from the pediatric floor along with volunteers and parents filled the room for the annual event. The decorations the children had made hung from the ceil-

ing: glittery stars, strings of red and green paper garland, candy canes and snowmen danced above them.
An artificial tree adorned with lights and childlike
wooden ornaments stood in a corner, its branches spilling over with tinsel, small gifts for the children stacked
beneath.

Laughter and excited voices drifted around her, helping Hannah forget her earlier worries.

"Dr. Hannah," a little blond girl on crutches said,
"is Santa Claus really coming?"

"That's what I heard," Hannah said with a wide grin.

One of the volunteers played the piano while a cancer
specialist burst out in song to lead the children. Soon
the crowd joined in singing a litany of Christmas tunes,
including the children's favorites, *Rudolph the Red-
Nosed Reindeer* and *Frosty the Snowman.*

Finally, the head of pediatrics stood up and clapped
her hands. "How about some refreshments, kids?"

The children yelled an emphatic yes. Simon, a small
boy in a wheelchair, raised his hand as the volunteers
passed out paper cups full of punch and plates of Christmas cookies. "When is Santa coming?"

Laughter sparkled in the pediatrician's eyes. "As a
matter of fact, I think I hear him now. Just listen." She
cupped her hand to her ear and the room grew quiet,
the children all leaning forward in anticipation.

Hannah glanced at the door, expecting to see her dear
father bound through any minute.

"Ho, ho, ho. Merry Christmas!" Santa Claus suddenly appeared, jingle bells ringing, boots stomping, his
voice ringing out through the room.

Only the voice didn't belong to her father.

Hannah gasped in surprise when she recognized
Jake's dark eyes twinkling from beneath a Santa hat that

had flopped over his forehead, his voice slightly muffled through the thick white beard.

"Jake?" she mouthed.

He grinned, a lopsided sexy-Santa grin that sent a shiver up her spine.

The children all clapped and yelled. "Santa Claus is here!"

"Look at his big belly!"

"He's got boots!"

"And presents!"

"Is your beard real?"

Jake gave his beard a yank, playing along with the children, then sailed through the crowd shouting, "Merry Christmas." He stopped to pat and shake the children's hands, bending to their level so he could greet each one, then pulled a gift from the burlap sack and placed it in their eager hands.

"And this one's for you," he said to Simon with a wink. "And here's to the pretty princess on her throne," he said, stooping to place a long box in the hands of a tiny little girl in a wheelchair.

Hannah's eyes misted over. He was supposed to give out the gifts from beneath the tree, but her father had obviously bought extra gifts, or maybe Jake had. Whatever the reason, the children squealed with delight as they opened the packages, parents and staff members roaming about to help and admiring the generous gifts and gathering the discarded wrapping paper. When his sack seemed empty, Hannah handed him the smaller presents from beneath the trees, packages filled with art paper and crayons for each of the kids, and Jake passed those out as well.

Tammy, a toddler who'd recently broken her leg when she'd jumped from a table pretending to fly like a superhero, wrapped her arms around Jake's neck. "Thank you, Santa. I wuv you."

Hannah saw Jake hug the little girl. "And I love you, too."

Her throat felt suddenly full of emotions. Jake might not know it, but he'd make a wonderful father. He gazed up and looked at her, the smile in his eyes so meaningful it took her breath away.

He gently eased away from the toddler. "I have a present here for one of your doctors, too," he said.

"Who?" the little girl shouted.

"Let's see!" some of the other kids yelled.

Jake moved toward Hannah, the heat flaring in his eyes obviously meant only for her. When he'd maneuvered through the crowded room, Hannah sensed all the children and volunteers and other doctors watching.

"Being Santa," Jake said, patting his red-velvet padded belly for emphasis so the kids laughed, "I have it on good authority that Dr. Hartwell once was a kid herself. A kid who collected dolls. But one year she forgot about those childish dreams and packed away her dolls."

"That's sad," the little girl in the wheelchair said.

"Well, Santa's here, hoping he can make Dr. Hartwell believe in dreams again."

"Yeah!" the children shouted.

"And Santa has a gift, something to add to her collection."

Hannah's pulse raced. Did Jake know she'd packed up the dolls and planned to give them away?

He pulled a box from his sack and handed it to Hannah. She stared at the package, wondering why Jake had chosen to bring her a doll after the way they'd parted.

Could he possibly have changed his mind about the two of them?

Then she remembered his phone call about the dog and the conversation with her grandmother and Mimi on Thanksgiving, when he'd claimed he wasn't a settle-down guy, didn't even own a dog. Was the pet a symbol he was ready to settle down? She'd thought him a big fearless man, but she knew his family history—had he been just as afraid of love as she had?

"Open it!" the little girl in the wheelchair shouted.

"Yeah, let's see!" the other kids yelled.

"Please open it, doc," Jake said softly.

Hannah's fingers trembled as she slipped them beneath the bright green paper and tore the edges. The paper fell away, and she lifted the lid of the box to find not one, but two dolls inside.

"The Tin Man from the *Wizard of Oz,*" she whispered, holding the doll up for the children to see.

Oohs and aahs filled the room.

"We're off to see the wizard," the children began to sing.

"And the Cowardly Lion." As she lifted the doll, she stared into Jake's eyes, questioning, yearning for an explanation.

Jake cleared his throat, his gaze locked with hers, his expression part embarrassment, part mischief. He addressed her and the children, "You kids remember the story of the *Wizard of Oz*?"

"Yeah, the Tin Man wanted a heart."

"And the Lion wanted courage."

"We're off to see the wizard," they began to chant the song again.

Jake pressed his hand over his heart, his gaze full of

emotions. "You have the Dorothy doll so I thought you should add these to the collection."

Hannah's eyes searched his.

"When the Lion and the Tin Man met Dorothy, they weren't whole. She helped them find the parts they were missing. Doc, you helped me find my heart, you helped me realize that it was empty without you. And you helped me see that all I needed was the courage to love someone and I would be whole."

"Jake—"

"He's Santa Claus!" Simon shouted.

"You also gave me a Christmas star so I could find my way home." He dropped to his knee and took her hand in his, kissing the top of her hand gently. Hannah's breath caught. The children giggled, along with the other doctors and volunteers.

"But Jake, it's too late, too much—"

He urged her to see the truth in his eyes. "Please Hannah. I followed that star and it led me back here. I want that home with you. I love you." He kissed her hand again.

"Will you marry me, doc?"

"I thought Santa already had a wife," Simon said.

Hannah laughed, tears slipping down her cheeks as she saw the truth in his eyes. He had been afraid, but he was willing to take the risk—and so should she. "I love you, too." She threw her arms around him, forgetting all her fears. "And yes, I'll marry you."

Jake lifted her in his arms and spun her around as the children laughed and squealed.

"Click your heels," a little girl shouted.

"You have to say 'There's no place like home' three times," another child yelled.

"But then they'll disappear and go to the North Pole," Simon said.

Jake stopped spinning and clicked his boots together three times as he repeated the line, "There's no place like home. There's no place like home. There's no place like home." Hannah broke into a grin as the kids chimed in.

"I don't know much about family," he admitted, dipping his head for a kiss. Will you teach me, doc?"

Hannah looped her arms around his neck. "You know the Hartwells are a pretty crazy bunch?"

"I know, and I love *all* of you."

She tousled his furry cap. "Then welcome to the Hartwell clan, honey. I think you're going to fit right in."

A FEW HOURS later, Hannah stared at the heirloom hope chest at the foot of her bed, smiling at the changes in her life since its arrival, then crawled into bed with Jake, ready to make mad passionate love to her soon-to-be husband, the man she intended to spend the rest of her life with. She finally understood what her grandmother had meant when she'd included the note about the rock—*Don't let the man you marry weigh you down.* Jake wouldn't weigh her down—he was rock hard in all the right places.

Epilogue

Mimi fluffed the train to Hannah's bridal gown while Alison adjusted the layers of netting from her veil. Deciding superstition and the folk legend might have something to do with her destiny after all, Hannah had worn her grandmother's dress and included something old, something new, something borrowed, something blue in her wedding theme, taking advantage of each of the items her grandmother had placed in her hope chest. The bride doll served as a centerpiece for the lace-draped gift table and the pearl ring gleamed from her right hand— she was saving her left ring finger for her wedding ring.

Her father stepped up and offered his arm, his gray suit and hot-pink tie a perfect accent to her sisters' rose-colored dresses and the roses that were scattered everywhere. Jake had insisted on red roses. They decorated the refreshment table, the red carpet on which she would walk, and the wedding arch of the gazebo where they would exchange their vows. Right on top of Pine Mountain. She and Jake had decided to marry at her grandmother's house in the old-fashioned gazebo in the backyard overlooking the beautiful countryside. Grammy Rose waved a dainty handkerchief from the front row of white chairs, her eyes twinkling with pleasure.

Soft strains of a guitar began, "I Will Always Love You," and her sisters took their places, beaming as they walked down the aisle. Hannah recognized several of her father's friends in attendance, along with a few doctors and nurses, including Tiffany, from the hospital. Even Jake's partner, Trevor Muldoon, showed up. And she was grateful Seth had decided to join them, too. But the biggest surprise of the day was her mother—she had shown up unexpectedly. Hannah still wasn't sure how she felt after not seeing her for so many years.

When the beautiful song had ended, Hannah emerged from behind the canopy and spotted Jake standing at the end of the walkway. Dressed in a black tux with his dark hair combed and a sexy grin on his face, he looked like a prince from one of her childhood stories. Finally, the guitar strummed the wedding march.

"Ready, hon?"

Hannah smiled at her father and squeezed his arm. "Yes, Dad. This time I'm ready."

The two of them walked slowly down the aisle together until they reached the gazebo, Hannah's gaze locking with Jake's as her father offered her to him in marriage. The preacher, Grammy's minister from Pine Mountain, offered a word of prayer, then began the service. "I understand you'd like to say your own vows."

Hannah and Jake nodded. Silence descended on the meadow, the fragrance of spring grass and flowers filling the air with the promise of rebirth.

Jake folded her hands between his own and kissed them gently, then began, "I came to Sugar Hill as an imposter. A man who knew nothing of love or family or belonging. And you, Hannah Hartwell, taught me how to open my heart. I will love and honor and cherish you as long as I live."

Hannah had to swallow against the tears. She pressed Jake's hands to her heart. "As a little girl, I used to dream of being rescued by a prince someday. But then one day I forgot how to dream. You, Jake Tippins, brought me out of that shell, forced me to take a chance and not be afraid. You are my prince—you rescued me from a life without dreams. I will love and honor and cherish you all the days of my life."

The minister completed the ceremony by having them exchange rings. Hannah smiled at the solid row of diamonds in the simple gold band she and Jake had chosen, knowing the wedding band would complement her grandmother's heirloom ring. She'd finally told Jake the story about how the ring had brought them together. One day she would pass the priceless antique on to her own daughter.

The minister continued, "I now pronounce you husband and wife. You may kiss the bride."

Jake swept her into his arms and kissed her to the sound of clapping and laughter. Several minutes later, when everyone had hugged them and offered congratulations, Grammy Rose stepped up to greet them. Hannah saw Seth talking to Mimi in the corner and was grateful they could all be friends.

Grammy Rose cupped Jake's handsome strong face between her gnarled wrinkled hands and kissed his cheek. "You take care of my granddaughter, you hear me? She's a special one."

"I know that, and I will," Jake assured her.

Grammy Rose patted his arm. "My, my, he's got some muscles on him, child."

Hannah laughed at the coy expression in her grandmother's eyes. "By the way, I always meant to ask you,

Hannah, how did you like that stripper I sent to your bachelorette party?''

"You sent Zorro, Gram?" Hannah asked.

"Yes, was he as good as they say?"

Hannah blushed.

"He was fabulous," Alison and Mimi said in unison.

"What about Zorro?" Jake's dark eyebrows arched teasingly, but his voice held a note of possessiveness. Maybe jealousy.

"He was a stripper," Mimi explained.

Jake dragged Hannah into his arms. "Well, my wife won't need Zorro around anymore. Now she has me."

Alison whistled suggestively. "You know, Hannah, Jake's a cop. I bet he'll know what to do with those handcuffs."

Hannah laughed again. "Alison!"

Jake nuzzled her neck with kisses. "I certainly do. And I can't wait to get you alone to show you."

"You've got your work cut out for you, Jake." Mimi gestured toward a bright silver gift bag sitting by the wedding cake. "But I packed you a honeymoon goody bag for starters. All kinds of erotic—"

"You don't have to explain, Mimi," Hannah warned.

Jake chuckled. "Don't worry, Mimi. I think Hannah and I can figure things out." He bent her across his arm for a long tender kiss, eliciting sighs and cheers from the family.

Hannah finally caught her breath and noticed her grandmother's eyes twinkling with appreciation. "Yes, ma'am, Hannah," Grammy said with a wink. "I couldn't have chosen a more perfect husband for you if I'd handpicked him myself."

Fall in Love with...

MEN
in UNIFORM

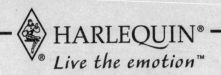

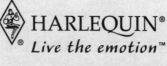

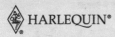

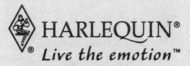

HARLEQUIN®
INTRIGUE®

BREATHTAKING ROMANTIC SUSPENSE

Shared dangers and passions lead to electrifying
romance and heart-stopping suspense!

Every month, you'll meet six new heroes
who are guaranteed to make your spine tingle
and your pulse pound. With them you'll enter
into the exciting world of Harlequin Intrigue—
where your life is on the line
and so is your heart!

THAT'S INTRIGUE—
ROMANTIC SUSPENSE
AT ITS BEST!

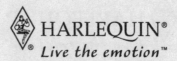

MEN *in* **UNIFORM**

Courteous, courageous and commanding—
these heroes lay it all on the line for the
people they love in more than fifty stories about
loyalty, bravery and romance.
Don't miss a single one!